"You've got a lot of nerve!"

Sly's chest quaked with laughter, and he peered at Cassie through the narrow half-moons of his eyes. "Me? What did I do?"

Cassie slapped the tangled strands of hair out of her face and stood up. "I don't want to discuss it."

Pursing his lips to fight his grin, he propped himself up on an elbow and shrugged. "All right. Guess you just woke up on the wrong side of the bed."

"You better believe I woke on the wrong side of the bed! *Your* side, you—"

"All I did was hold you," he said in a whispery, broken voice.

"You shouldn't have. You had no business—"

"You're my wife," he said with slow emphasis.

"I'm not your wife!" she flung back. "I'm part of your past and that's all. There is nothing between us anymore. Nothing!"

Dear Reader,

Although our culture is always changing, the desire to love and be loved is a constant in every woman's heart. Silhouette Romances reflect that desire, sweeping you away with books that will make you laugh and cry, poignant stories that will move you time and time again.

This year we're featuring Romances with a playful twist. Remember those fun-loving heroines who always manage to get themselves into tricky predicaments? You'll enjoy reading about their escapades in Silhouette Romances by Brittany Young, Debbie Macomber, Annette Broadrick and Rita Rainville.

We're also publishing Romances by many of your all-time favorites such as Ginna Gray, Dixie Browning, Laurie Paige and Joan Hohl. Your overwhelming reaction to these authors has served as a touchstone for us, and we're pleased to bring you more books with Silhouette's distinctive medley of charm, wit and—above all—*romance*. I hope you enjoy this book, and the many stories to come.

Sincerely,

Rosalind Noonan
Senior Editor
SILHOUETTE BOOKS

TERRI HERRINGTON
Lovers' Reunion

Silhouette *Romance*

Published by Silhouette Books New York

America's Publisher of Contemporary Romance

For the Wingfield High School Class of 1975, and
For Don, my high-school sweetheart

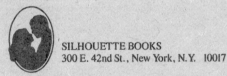

SILHOUETTE BOOKS
300 E. 42nd St., New York, N.Y. 10017

Copyright © 1986 by Terri Herrington

ISBN: 0-373-08416-1

First Silhouette Books printing February 1986

America's Publisher of Contemporary Romance

Printed in the U.S.A.

Books by Terri Herrington

Silhouette Romance

Blue Fire #318
Lovers' Reunion #416

TERRI HERRINGTON

resides with her supportive husband and two-year-old daughter in Louisiana, but she has lived in eight states and spent part of her childhood in Holland. She feels that falling in love is the most special feeling in the world, one that she experiences anew each time she writes or reads a romance.

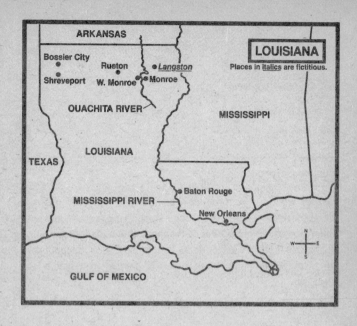

Chapter One

It was too late to change her mind.

Standing beneath the vent that blew cool air into the rich auburn hair draping her shoulders, Cassie Farrell clutched her purse with a trembling hand. She watched through the airport window as the jet rolled to a stop. Leaning her forehead against the glass, warmed by the July sun descending in the west, Cassie closed her eyes and tried to concentrate on slowing her pulse before she came face to face with Sly for the first time in a year.

Silly, she chided herself as she blew out a held breath and turned her back to the travelers coming from the tunnel to awaiting relatives, friends, lovers. It wasn't as if they were strangers. She'd been married to the man for eleven years. There had been a time in her life when a simple expression between them could translate a mood, when a sentence begun did not have to be finished, when her very thoughts had spilled over for Sly to pick up in her eyes. They had been transparent to each other once; everything hinged on her not being transparent now.

Taking a deep breath, Cassie ran a hand through her hair and turned toward the scattering passengers. Her hand froze when, through the flurry of passing strangers, she saw him standing still, blocking the flow of traffic, his blue eyes trained on her.

Letting her hair cascade around her face, Cassie lifted her hand in a wave, unable to help the smile that was breaking across her face. If he had changed since she'd seen him last, it was only in subtle ways that refined and matured him. New lines added character to the night-blue eyes she had drowned in more than once, and the dimples in his cheeks were deeper now, more permanent fixtures in the jaws that were never completely free of the shadow of stubble. For a moment she lost reality, and remembered only the bond between them in spite of their broken marriage—a bond rooted in childhood, entwined with memories of a lifetime incomplete without each other, more than lovers, more than friends. It seemed fitting, given the circumstances of the past, that she would be here for him now, sharing a lie by choice, despite her misgivings. She wondered why Amanda, the woman he was currently involved with, had gone along with Sly's scheme. Perhaps she had counted on Sly's buried feelings, as Cassie had counted on her own. Now she realized she had underestimated the powers of the past.

Slinging his duffel bag over his shoulder, Sly swept a careless hand through his dark hair and pushed through the crowd to where she stood. "Cass." The word, formed more with his breath than his deep voice, brought back a flood of memories that immediately put Cassie on the defensive. Without warning, he slid his hand under her hair to the back of her neck and pressed a kiss on her forehead. "Sexy as ever," he breathed, leveling his eyes on the apricot neckline dipping to her breasts.

"Sly, please," Cassie said with irritation, stepping away from his touch and schooling her green eyes to hide the whirlwind of emotions that was dizzying her. "How was your flight?"

Grinning at her exasperation, he dropped his hand. "Typical. How was yours?"

"Okay," she answered, pretending to be distracted by the noisy activity around them. She glanced at her watch. "We'd better hurry if we're going to make our connection. Your flight was a little late." She began walking away as she spoke, but Sly grabbed her arm and turned her around to face him.

"Cass, don't be afraid to look at me," he said earnestly. "It's just me."

"I'm not afraid," she said. "We're in a hurry. That's all."

"We've got a minute," he argued, still holding her arm as if his touch had some magical power that could turn back time and make the charade more plausible. "Before we go I want you to know how much I appreciate this."

Cassie hardened her eyes at the reminder of the favor that had brought them together. "You told me on the phone," she said.

He slid his hand up her neck, and his fingers closed gently over her soft earlobe. He traced the curve of her ear, turning the gold studs with his fingers as he lowered his face closer to hers to emphasize his words. "I mean it, though. It was a lot to ask, and you could have refused—"

"I did refuse," she reminded him.

He grinned, tipping her face to his. "Only three times," he said. "The fourth time you gave in right away."

Cassie couldn't fight her smile, for the sparkle in his eyes was contagious. "By the fourth time I'd have agreed to anything to get you off the phone."

Sly cocked a brow, rounding his lips and whistling under his breath. "Wish I'd known. I'd have asked for a little more."

Losing her smile at the bold remark, Cassie again stepped back until his hand lost contact with her face. "You wouldn't have gotten any more. I'm doing this for your grandmother, Sly. Not for you."

Lifting his hand in a gesture of defeat, Sly cocked a brow and nodded, his eyes losing some of their luster. "I'll consider that a warning," he said grimly. Dropping his head, he swept his hand through his hair once more, leaving it ruffled and tousled. One side of the crisp, white collar of his shirt was caught under the shoulder of his sport coat, and following a reflex, Cassie reached up to straighten it. His eyes met hers when her thumb brushed his neck, and quickly she pulled her hand back.

"We'd better go," he said, glancing past her into the throng.

Nodding silently, she led him out of the waiting area into the busy thoroughfare of the Atlanta, Georgia, airport.

Their connecting flight to their hometown of Langston, Louisiana, was a gate not far from where they had met, and few words were exchanged as they reached it. Sly's entrance, as it had always done, drew the attention of several women lining up to board. She wondered if he noticed, for the natural, unselfconscious way he wove through the people with his hand on Cassie's arm made him seem oblivious to the stares. It was part of his charisma, Cassie thought. Part of what made him so attractive.

When they had boarded the plane and found their seats in first class, a luxury on which Sly had insisted, the stewardess approached them, smiling cheerfully. "Enjoy your flight, Mr. and Mrs. Farrell," she said. "Let me know if you need anything."

Sly watched Cassie take her seat, her eyes hardening at the innocent, understandable assumption of the flight attendant. She hooked her seat belt, letting her eyes drift to the window where she could see the luggage outside being loaded beneath the plane.

"Well, you do still use my name," he said in a low voice after he had secured his bag in an overhead compartment and settled next to her. His shoulder pressed boldly against hers, but moving away seemed pointless.

"It's *my* name," Cassie corrected in a low, placid voice. "I've used it professionally for years, and I saw no point in complicating things by changing it."

Sly rubbed at his grin. "Good point." He leaned his head back into the seat and tapped his jaw with a long finger. Although she was still looking out the window, she felt his eyes on her, burning her with nostalgic intimacy, stirring emotions she wanted buried. Hoping it would end his scrutiny, she met his gaze.

"You know, you're still the most beautiful girl at Redmond High," he said in a soft rumble, his teasing eyes molding her like gentle, caressing fingers.

Cassie set her arm on the wide rest between them, a halfhearted wisp of a smile softening her lips. "Sara Klein was the most beautiful girl at Redmond High," she reminded him.

His finger went to the back of her hand, and she watched, motionless, as he traced the small bone leading to her middle knuckle. "Not to me, she wasn't."

The plane's engines began to turn, and Cassie felt herself rolling backward in time as the jet turned around to prepare for takeoff. Sly continued his seduction of her fingers, then settled his hand over hers, his thumb feathering the side of her hand. "Would you have come back for the class reunion if I hadn't asked you?" Instead of looking at her when he posed the soft question, he watched the hand that seemed more in tune with the truth.

She nodded. "Probably. I miss everybody, and I wanted to see them. But not like this." Her eyes were on their hands, too, watching almost objectively as most subjective feelings coursed through her at their gentle contact. He had always been an expert lover, and the fact that he was no longer her own had not changed things. She knew his methods, but the knowledge was no defense against the erotic touch of his fingers. When the plane left the ground, she was scarcely aware of it.

The flight attendant made her announcements and took their orders for drinks, the pilot made his verbal introductions, the No Smoking signs flashed their sanctions. Through it all, Sly toyed with her fingers, keeping the magic alive, building it until it would spellbind her. After a while, he lifted her hand and studied the bare fingers, soft and pliant as the first time he'd held them. "I've been debating whether to ask you this," he said quietly, threading his fingers through hers in such a natural way that the thought of pulling back never occurred to her. "But since we're trying to pretend we're still married, I guess it isn't that unreasonable."

"What?" she asked. Her own fingers curled through his.

"The ring. I was wondering if you'd mind wearing the ring."

Cassie hadn't been aware of the breath she had been holding in her lungs while he'd fondled her hand, but a long, weary sigh escaped at his request. She had almost forgotten the ring. They had never spoken of it since she'd left it on the dresser amid his loose change, comb, and pocket knife the morning she'd left. It had been like severing the holding link in the chain of their marriage. She did not want to wear it again.

"Lots of married couples don't wear rings," she answered. "I don't think it's necessary."

"Ordinarily, it wouldn't be," Sly said, the importance of his request becoming evident in the pleading blue of his eyes and the deeper strokes of his thumb on her hand. "But the people who know us—the ones who were there when we got married and know how much those rings meant—they'll wonder."

"Let them wonder," she said. "They have no reason to think anything has happened to our marriage."

"My grandmother will wonder," he said, as if that changed everything. And it did.

Cassie swallowed and pulled back her hands. His grandmother, the fragile old woman for whom this whole charade was taking place, would notice the absence of the rings the moment they got off the plane. The simple gold bands, which had once been more precious to Cassie than diamonds or emeralds, had been passed down through generations of Sly's family. "Do you have it with you?" she asked in a whisper.

In answer, Sly reached to his inside coat pocket and pulled out the two bands. Picking the smaller one off his palm, he held it up for her. "I had it cleaned for you," he said.

A fresh feeling of loss overwhelmed Cassie, and swallowing back the mist that was filling her throat, she propped her right elbow on the rest by the window and set her chin on her hand. "I'm a little surprised you haven't given it to Amanda," she said, choosing her words carefully to avoid sounding bitter.

"Amanda?" he asked, a guarded frown transforming his features. "How do you know about Amanda?"

Cassie shrugged. "I see Frank from time to time when he comes through town," she said, referring to a mutual friend who lived in Chicago. "He told me about her."

Sly breathed an annoyed sigh. "Ah, yes. Frank. He keeps me pretty well informed of your love life, too."

Cassie didn't answer. Nothing Frank told him could have been significant. After all, she hadn't had any serious involvement since Sly. She only wished he could say the same. An unwelcome memory invaded her thoughts, and she closed her eyes, recalling the newspaper article Frank had brought her with a photo of Amanda announcing her engagement to Sly, less than a week ago. Strange, she thought, that Sly wasn't taking this opportunity to break the news of the divorce and engagement, rather than continuing with the lie that kept them married in their families' eyes.

"It's your ring," Sly said, cutting into her thoughts. "I wouldn't give it to anyone else." He waited, watching her face for a response. "Please wear it, Cass. It's just for a couple of days," he prodded softly. "I'll wear mine, too."

Taking a broken breath, Cassie turned back to him, knowing that she could no more deny him this than she could deny her heart another beat. "I guess if we have to do this, we should do it right."

"I think so," he whispered, still holding the ring.

With trembling reluctance, Cassie surrendered her left hand. She felt the tremor in his own fingers as he slid the ring over hers, then held it there a moment, turning it around, studying it as if trying to recall the way it had looked before. The lines between his dark brows told her he was struggling, too, with the loss of what they'd shared. The loss born of their inability to share.

Cassie drew back her hand, breaking the spell, when she saw the flight attendant approaching with the tray carrying their drinks. Enclosing the other ring in his fist, Sly took both drinks and set them in their holders within the arm rest. Then, without ceremony, he slipped his own ring on and picked up his drink again.

"I still don't like it," Cassie said, watching the liquid swirl in her glass with the movement of the plane. "We should have told them by now. Faced up to it."

Sly took another drink and peered over the rim of his glass to the seat in front of him. "We've been all through it. We agreed."

Sighing, Cassie leaned her head against the window and watched the clouds hovering in the darkening sky, trying to absorb some of their serenity. He was right, of course. They had agreed not to tell their families of their divorce. For a year they had successfully lived in different states, while their families believed they were both still living in Chicago. For a year Sly had forwarded her mail from home. For a year Cassie had called home weekly, just to make certain that her parents had no need of calling her. And on the few occasions when they had called, Sly had simply explained that she was away on a business trip and had gotten in touch with her in New York.

But the deceit had been necessary. Their divorce, the first in either of their large, thriving families, would have shaken their family members, starting a campaign of meddling and manipulation aimed at getting the two back together. No one would have been able to keep the breakup a secret from Sasha, the grandmother who adored both Sly and Cassie. And the disappointment might literally have killed her.

Cassie closed her eyes, pretending to sleep—wishing for sleep—as unsought memories of the beloved old woman's struggle with death came back to her. Her heart attack had been a reaction to the death of the baby that Cassie had wanted for nine years and carried for nine months. The stillbirth had been a shock, laying sorrow and grief and anger over them like a smothering shroud. After a few months the old woman had recovered, unlike Cassie and Sly, whose separate, silent anguish had torn them apart. Their marriage had died with the baby they had tried for most of their marriage to conceive, and neither of them had found the strength to revive it. Neither had had the will to hang on.

But even after Sasha's recovery, they had agreed to keep the secret of their divorce a while longer. There seemed no point in destroying the old woman's faith in the love she had so strongly believed in when they were young. There seemed no reason to risk provoking another heart attack. And the decision had been as much Cassie's as it had been Sly's. Sasha, whom Cassie had loved since she was five years old, had made Cassie's wedding gown. Their union had represented all that was good in the world to the old woman, and each stitch had been lovingly placed, as if it alone would be strong enough to build the foundation of marriage.

Who would have dreamed then that they'd one day wind up here, like this—two separate lives, joining together to protect a lie?

Opening her eyes, Cassie saw that Sly's wistful eyes were watching her.

"I thought you were sleeping," he said.

She shook her head. "Just thinking."

"Nervous?"

She laughed. "Because we're going back to our fifteen-year class reunion pretending to be married when we're not? Nah."

He smiled. "Nothing to worry about. I've been talking to Jerry," he said, referring to his best friend from school and the class's vice-president. "It sounds like the reunion might be fun."

"In spite of all this," Cassie said, "I am looking forward to it."

A reminiscent sparkle flared in Sly's eyes, and he leaned closer to her. "If only we could really go back." He seemed to catch himself, and his smile waned. "I mean, to our youth. To the uncomplicated years of adolescence."

"Uncomplicated?" Cassie asked. "I remember quite a few complications back then. Remember the time you wrapped Mr. Blumenthal's house in toilet paper, and he'd just had it painted, and it rained and the tissue got all mixed in with the paint . . . ?"

Sly covered his face and grimaced. "You're right. I guess my life has never been uncomplicated."

"Never," she said, her lips curling derisively.

He watched her smile brighten her eyes, and the light was reflected in his own. Lifting his hand, he pushed a strand of hair away from her face, letting his fingers take their time combing out the silky web. Nervously, Cassie swept it back herself, pulling it from his fingers.

"Adulthood," he said in a bland voice, dropping his hand. "Every phase of it comes as a bigger surprise."

Feeling as if she'd drowned the fiery source of her warmth, Cassie looked out the window where the night lights of Louisiana were coming into view. "No one ever gave guarantees," she muttered more to herself than to him.

Leaning forward, he looked over her shoulder to the lights below. His voice came behind her ear, deep and soft like the roaring engines. "Funny how we thought we had them."

She sat back and closed her eyes. Wanting not to love him, wanting not to remember, wanting not to hurt after the events that had taken attention from their loss, she bit her lip. There had been moments over the past year when she'd desperately needed him back, when memories even stronger than pain, and love bigger than heartache, had made the problems seem smaller. Once, after the divorce, she had even gone to him. Finding him with another woman, she had learned firsthand that there had never been guarantees. "We were wrong," she said in answer to his comment now. "Naive."

"Naive," he repeated with a mirthless chuckle, tapping a finger on his arm rest.

The lights below them, flickering like multicolored candles in a sanctuary, grew closer. Cassie became more uneasy. "We're almost there," she whispered.

Sly looked over her shoulder. "Home," he said in a voice tinged with awe.

The sound of the word caused a strange swelling in her throat, and Cassie swallowed and bit her knuckle. Somehow, home had gotten lost in the shuffle. There hadn't been one for her since she'd given up on their marriage. And now, here they were, dragging themselves back through the past, back to the town they'd left to build their own home, their own life. How could she bear it?

The plane began its descent, and Cassie's fingernails bit into her seat. It was insane, she thought, pretending they were still in love. It would never work.

But it was too late to change the plan now. Too late.

As if sensing her fears, Sly encased her hands in his own. "It'll be all right, babe," he said, the way he had said it during her labor, before they'd known that the baby was in distress. But nothing had ever been all right again.

She didn't pull away, for she needed the strength of his touch, even if it was just for a moment. "I don't think I can do this," she whispered.

"We have to do it," Sly said, looking past her through the window as the plane's wheels touched down, jarring them slightly. She could see in his eyes that he was having his own doubts. "We'll do it for Sasha."

Slowly, the feeling of purpose fell over her, and Cassie nodded her head with resolution. "For Sasha," she whispered as the plane slowed on the long runway.

Chapter Two

Except for the other passengers following behind them, hurrying in anticipation, the ramp leading to where their families were waiting was dim and empty. Cassie felt as if she were backstage at a Broadway production, preparing to walk out on stage, the star who'd forgotten her lines. Her stomach churned, and her throat felt dry. She glanced at Sly, who was watching the floor as if it were about to open and swallow him. They hadn't been home since before her pregnancy, and Cassie wasn't certain why she had avoided it so adamantly. Perhaps it was the dread of too much change. How could the past be comforting when Sly was no longer a part of her present? She wondered what Sly's reasons for staying away had been. He had called her before each holiday, asking her plans about going back to Langston. Each time she had found another reason not to go home, and he had matched it with excuses of his own. This last time, however, he had made up his mind to go back, and he had been set on persuading her to join him.

Just before they reached the end of the ramp, Sly paused and stepped aside to let the other passengers go by. Cassie stopped, too, and turned to face him. He ran a rugged hand through his hair, first smoothing it away from his forehead, then unconsciously messing it up again. His pensive eyes were soft and questioning. His throat moved as he set his hand on her shoulder, massaging it gently. "You ready?"

Not at all certain, Cassie straightened the light jacket over her sundress and nodded. Sly heaved a deep sigh, and lowered his hand to her waist. "All right, let's do it." His voice was calm, no more than a whisper, and his hand cupped her side in a possessive, reassuring manner that filled the raw need she had not been aware of.

They were barely inside the airport when a familiar clatter of happy voices resounded around them. Genuine smiles broke across both their faces as family members swept them into the tight circle of hugs and kisses, tears and laughter, shouts and whispers. Embracing both of her parents, Cassie closed her eyes and realized she had owed it to herself to get back to her foundations.

Her exhilaration was pierced by a sharp, hoarse voice behind her. "Shame on you! Shame on both of you!"

Turning from her parents, she saw Sly's wiry little grandmother with one arm imprisoning him and the other held out for Cassie. The woman's shaky arms made her seem even more frail, and biting her smile,

Cassie stepped into the circle of her warmth. "Sasha!"

"Why should we be ashamed, Grandma?" Sly asked, looking down at the woman who waved an annoyed hand in his direction.

"Waiting all this time to come back here. You two should live here. It's your home. How can we keep up with anything you do when you live all the way across the world?"

Laughter filled Cassie's throat for the first time in months.

"Chicago is not across the world," Sly reminded the taunting woman. Eyes the lambent blue of sunwarmed sea sparked forgotten memories, and the sight of the dimples on his cheeks when he grinned reminded Cassie of a time long past. Strange, she thought, that she should only now let herself really see him, with the protective buffers of family surrounding her to help with the stirrings.

"It might as well be," Sasha goaded. "You might as well live on the moon. Now tell me about everything." She slipped her arms through each of theirs and started walking as the others fell into step behind them. Before either of them could speak, she narrowed her eyes and studied Cassie. "I know what *you've* been doing, Cassandra. You've been working yourself to death. You work too hard, hopping all over the country buying department stores."

Cassie laughed and caught Sly's "I told you it was worth it" wink over the old woman's head. "I don't buy department stores, Sasha. I am a buyer *for* a chain of department stores. And how do you know I work too hard?"

"How do I know?" the matriarch repeated, pulling her arm from Sly and shaking a reproachful finger at Cassie. "Because you are never there when I call. Always away on business, or still at the office, or tied up in a meeting." Cassie's smile faded slightly, along with Sly's. She had known the lie would confront them, but she hadn't expected it so soon. "You're too young to be a workaholic."

Before Cassie could reply, Sasha's attention had switched to Sly. "And you! Have you never heard of delegating authority? A man who owns his own company ought at least to have someone he can leave the business with so he can come home and visit his old grandmother once in a while."

Sly's broad grin returned and he laughed aloud and winked at Cassie again. "I'm here, aren't I?"

"Yes," the old woman sighed, patting his hand, then reaching back for Cassie. "Yes, you're here. You're finally here." Lifting her shoulders in a gesture of suppressed excitement, she slapped Sly's face playfully. "You get more handsome every year. Just like your grandfather." Cassie repressed a smile, recalling a conversation so many years ago, when Sasha had proclaimed, "Well, I know you aren't marrying him for his money, so it must be for his looks. And I can't say I blame you for that since I married his grandfather for the same reason."

Things had seemed so simple then.

Sasha chattered nonstop, along with the rest of their family, as they made their way downstairs to pick up their luggage. When they discovered that one of Cassie's smaller bags was missing, she refused to report it for fear that everyone would notice the different points of origin. Having convinced the relatives that it would be easier to do it by phone, the two families, close friends for generations, led them to the van they had all ridden in.

"How did you get twelve people in this thing?" Sly asked while he helped Sasha in.

With giggling demonstrations, the others crowded into the small space, settling on the floor and doubling up in seats and on the sofa bed at the rear. Cassie, who was in conversation with her younger sister, was one of the last ones in. Climbing into the dark vehicle, she looked around for a seat and laughed. "I think I'll take a cab."

"There's always room for you," Sly said, catching her by the hips and pulling her onto his lap. Before she could react, her sister was inside, closing the door and settling at her feet, preventing her from getting up without drawing attention.

In the darkness, Sly was smiling up at her, his smoky-blue eyes daring her to object. She felt his breath on her neck, smelled the minty scent of his breath as he wet his lips. Dragging her eyes from his, she reflected that he had not lost his touch. But how could he? she reminded herself. He had stayed in practice.

Forcing her senses back to the world around her, Cassie caught the pungent smell of cinnamon. "Am I dreaming?" she asked the old woman who beamed at the surprise on her face.

Sasha's hoarse laughter rang out above the van's rumbling engine. "I baked your favorite this afternoon," she announced, unwrapping the cinnamon rolls in their warm pan. "Thought you might be hungry on the way home."

Cassie knew that happiness and food were synonymous in Sasha's mind, but the special memory-invoking scent of the rolls made her mouth water. "I'd kiss you if I could reach you," she said, reaching for one of the warm, sticky treasures.

Sly leaned forward with Cassie. Still holding her firmly with one arm, he reached for his own roll, but his hand was slapped away. "They're not for you, Sylvester!" Sasha said, and Sly winced at the sharp use of his given name. "They're for Cassie."

A roaring protest descended on the old woman from all the passengers, and laughing, Cassie said, "Ah, let them have some. I can settle for one if you'll bake me more later."

With feigned vexation at her hungry crew, Sasha passed the pan around.

Sly sat back as Cassie brought the morsel to her lips, cupping her hand beneath it to catch the crumbs and dripping frosting. She closed her eyes when the taste of home wrapped her in nostalgic sensations—from the sticky feel of frosting between her fingers, to the warm, moist melting in her mouth, to the possessive feel of Sly's arms around her hips, his heavy-lidded eyes watching while she ate. Everything seemed as it should be. Painfully so.

Opening her eyes, she smiled down at Sly, whose close attention to her enjoyment had caused him to miss claiming his own roll. His head leaned back on the high seat, and even in the darkness the deep crystalline color of his eyes was clear, honest, as he gazed up at her. The intensity of his serene study of her caused her heart to struggle for another beat, and she froze with the roll at her lips. As if in slow motion, Sly's arms closed tighter around her and his head rose until his lips were inches from hers. Breath was trapped and blood rushed in a furious emotional onslaught when his teeth closed over the pastry, his moist lips brushing the trembling fingers that held it for him. His eyes burned into her as he chewed.

Wrenching her eyes back to the roll, which suddenly seemed tasteless in comparison to the promise on his lips, Cassie took a final bite, then dropped the rest into his mouth.

Before she could pull her hand away, Sly had captured it. His tongue, soft as wet velvet, sucked the frosting from her fingertips, lingering over each finger, his eyes smouldering and heavy, searing her soul.

The other family members were forgotten for a moment—for in the brief span of seconds it took for Cassie's vital functions to recover, the whole world froze in some oblique time frame that had no bearing on anything passing between them. But as quickly as the lightning bolt of fantasy struck, the thunderous roar of chattering voices invaded again and she pulled her fingers away, turning her eyes back to Sasha, who was basking in the praise of all who had tasted the rolls.

Sly licked the taste from his lips, and though she did not look at him, Cassie could still feel the stirring warmth of his eyes on her, until someone demanded his attention.

Relieved that his father had saved her from the penetration of his thoughts delving into her own, Cassie listened to his answer concerning the workings of his computer consulting company, an enterprise Cassie had helped him conceive.

"We're doing very well," Sly was saying. "Last year's profits were double those of the year before. And this year we've picked up three major accounts already for national companies based in Chicago." His thumb seemed to be creeping up her ribs, but Cassie told herself it was imagination, since his face showed no sign of interest in anything other than the subject of conversation.

"Much of it was word of mouth," he was saying, "and some of our clients were so grateful that we were able to get some valuable stock in their companies..." As he spoke, his hand moved subtly under the peach-colored cloth of her jacket to her bare back, where her sundress swooped to her waist except for the crisscrossed straps. Cassie caught her breath at the contact of his hand on her bare flesh, but his absorption in answering his family's questions continued to convince her the move had been an accident.

"What about the cotton? Did you lose it?" Sly was asking his parents, pursuing a new conversation about their farm. Slowly, his thumb moved up her rib cage and slipped under the cloth draping her sides.

Suddenly aware that Sly knew exactly what he was doing, Cassie let her back go rigid, but his arm across her lap only tightened. "I hear Chester invented a new tool for the harvest," he went on, seemingly unaffected. "How does it work?"

His hand was rising, his thumb caressing the outer swell of her naked breast. The fold of her jacket and the cover of darkness hid his seduction from the others. Cassie swallowed, but her concentration did nothing to slow the breaths threatening to strangle her as his thumb swept over her budded nipple, circling it, savoring it, using it as the point where he could send his desire shooting through her intellect and driving right into her instinct.

His voice grew raspy as he continued talking, and Cassie felt his hand trembling over her aroused breast. "I know a guy in the research department at Trasters who might be interested . . ."

Beneath her, she felt his own arousal, and closing her eyes, she desperately fought the desire burning like a nuclear core, surging through her like a red alert. His breathing grew quicker as he seemed to listen attentively to his brother, and his arm across her lap became heavier, binding her more firmly to him.

Cassie wasn't aware that her fingers were digging into his leg until he pried them loose.

"What do you think, Cassie?" her mother was asking, bringing her reeling back to earth as if she'd leaped from a ten-story building to stop this madness. Sly's grinning eyes came back to her, eloquent with promise.

"About what?" she asked in a shaky voice.

"About Barbara's ceremony. Do you think she should risk an outdoor wedding?"

"An outdoor wedding?" Cassie repeated, trying to bring her thoughts back into the focus of reality. "I don't know."

"Yours was outside," Barbara reminded her, as if her indecisiveness threatened to ruin her case with her mother.

Clearing her throat, Cassie shifted on Sly's lap so that she was sitting only on the edge of one leg, and

leaned toward her sister to put as much distance between herself and Sly as possible. "What do you have
in mind?"

Sly's mother spoke up. "You're welcome to use the
farm, like Sly and Cassie did. I've never seen a more
beautiful wedding."

"Never," Barbara sighed. "I've always wanted a
wedding like that."

A new reason for quiet fell over Cassie as the van
threaded its way through town, the lights from passing cars and streetlamps casting bars of brightness and
shadows over Sly's face. His hand held her arm gently
now, as if to tell her he felt the shame of the charade,
too. Neither contributed to the anecdotes being exchanged about their wedding.

Cassie felt desperately relieved when the van left the
paved road and journeyed down the gravel street
leading to the home where Sly had grown up, and her
own childhood home less than a mile away. Cassie had
lived there with him when they'd first married, and
there they had stayed until both had finished college
and Cassie had been offered the job in Chicago, which
had prompted their move.

"I can't believe we're here," Sly said with delight
when the van doors slid open and the sight of the
large, beloved house greeted him. One by one, the
passengers dropped from the van.

"Just like I promised on the phone, I've boiled
some crawfish," his father drawled. "Bet you haven't
had any of that in Illinois. It's out back, ready to be
devoured. Everybody go in and get a box to eat them
in, and we'll take care of your luggage."

Sly smiled and watched as everyone started toward the house, and behind her, Cassie heard him say, "Just leave the suitcases in the van. Cass and I have a suite at the Langston Inn, so we'll be leaving after we eat."

It hadn't occurred to her until that moment that his family might not allow them to stay in the hotel, where they had agreed to rent a large suite with two separate bedrooms. "You'd better take that up with your grandmother," his father said. "She's been fussing over that room of yours since she heard you were coming home."

Cassie's heart fell to her stomach, and a nagging voice in her head cried, "What next?" Hanging back while the others went into the house, she waited until Jasper had left them. Her eyes glowered as she stood face to face with Sly in the night.

"I guess you heard," Sly said, one of his dimples casting a slash of darkness on his cheek, the foreshadowing of a smile.

"I heard." She bit out the words. "And I have no intention of staying with you in this house. After the stunt you pulled in that van—"

"What stunt?" he asked, brows innocently raised.

"You know what I'm talking about!" she hissed. "I won't tolerate any more of it!"

Chuckling, Sly stepped toward her. "I really don't know what you're talking about, Cass." He reached for her shoulders. "You'll have to be more specific."

Shoving his hands away, Cassie took a step backward. "I'm warning you, Sly."

"What?" he asked, grinning intolerably and stepping toward her again.

"You will not treat me like that in front of other people!"

"Like my wife? I thought that was what I was supposed to do," he said easily.

Cassie's words grated through her teeth. "I'm not your wife, and I will not be pawed in public."

"Then I'll wait until we're alone," he whispered, capturing her in his arms and grinning down into her startled eyes. "Which we happen to be at this very moment." His face lowered slowly, testing her reaction.

Trapped into looking up at him, Cassie clenched her teeth and gave him a warning smile. "Kiss me and I'll bite your tongue off."

The threat struck Sly as amusing, and he let out a loud laugh, dropping her arms. "You win again," he conceded.

Feeling less than victorious, Cassie reached back into the van for her purse. "And I expect you to take care of our lodging situation as soon as possible. I have no intention of sharing a bed with you again."

"So I've suspected," he said, sliding his hands into his pockets and following her into the house, still grinning as if he knew something she didn't.

Cassie schooled her features to look less annoyed when she went into the brightness of the home where she and Sly had started their lives together. Photos of anxious young lovers decked the walls, a brutal reminder of the joy and innocent passion that had drawn the two of them together. Thinking back now, trying desperately to make some sense of her life, she recalled the euphoria of her wedding day, and the sleepless night that had followed. They had been so young, so untouched by life and death, so naive. And even now she could not deny that they'd been very much in love.

"You got new furniture," Sly was saying, and Cassie noted the dull edge in his voice.

"The other couch was a wreck," his mother answered. "I finally talked your father into something decent."

"I liked the old stuff," he said. He still smiled, but the light was gone from his eyes. His fingers moved across the back of the new sofa, and for the first time, Cassie saw the need in Sly's face to return home—not just in a physical sense, but in a nostalgic one, too. He missed those days, just as she did. And coming home wasn't going to bring them back.

The family was drifting out the back door to the tub of crawfish and boiled potatoes that awaited them. Although it was late, no one was too tired or too full for the Louisiana delicacy that took both hands to eat and soiled the clothes of even the most careful eater. The patio was surrounded by bug lights zapping the mosquitoes that, ordinarily, would have made it impossible for them to take advantage of the night. The lights lit the patio in a faint blue hue, and laughter and chatter, the music of home, rose above the sounds of crickets and tree frogs and the soft music coming from inside the house.

Barbara, a bundle of nerves because of her unsettled wedding plans, finished eating first. "Walk down to the pond with me, Cassie," she said. "I want to ask your advice about my wedding."

Thankful to escape Sly's scrutiny for a while, Cassie put aside her plate, washed her hands, and left the crowd. The night breeze cut the humidity, and the smell of fresh cut grass relaxed her like a sedative. "It's beautiful here," she said. "I'd forgotten."

"And the moon is full," Barbara pointed out. "I wish Paul didn't have to work tonight."

Cassie smiled. "Have you gotten your dress, yet?"

"Yes," Barbara exclaimed. "You'll have to see it. It's the most gorgeous gown I've ever seen, except for yours."

Cassie laughed. "You could have worn mine."

"I wanted my own," Barbara said. The words brought back memories of when they were younger, Cassie at seventeen and her sister at seven, lamenting about the outdated hand-me-downs she was forced to wear to school.

"I don't blame you," Cassie sighed.

"Do you think I should take Mrs. Farrell up on her offer? I can't think of a prettier place to have a wedding. And the Farrells seem like family to me, too."

Cassie tore a tall weed out of the ground as they reached the pond. "It's up to you. I know Martha meant it when she offered." The stars were a million tiny lights decorating the still water of the pond, an illusion less brilliant than the real thing, though just as intriguing. Picking up a rock, she tossed it into the water and watched the picture distort in circular ripples.

"Do you think you and Sly can make it back for the wedding? I know it's not that far off, but since you aren't staying that long this time—"

Cassie ripped the leaf off the weed she held. "I'll be here, Barbara. I can't speak for Sly, though. He might not be able to get away."

"I'll get away," a voice said from the shadows down the gravel path. Both women turned around to see Sly approaching them, a pine needle held between his teeth, his hair rumpling in the breeze. He had taken off his coat and rolled his sleeves up to just below his elbows, and the buttons of his shirt had been freed to halfway down his chest. "I wouldn't miss your wedding for the world, Barbara," he said pulling the straw out of his mouth and setting his arm on her shoulder.

"Cassie felt her lungs constricting. I didn't know you were there."

"Wasn't until just now," he said lightly. "But Barbara had a phone call from an admirer, and—"

"Paul's on the phone?" Barbara cut in.

"You'd better hurry," he said.

Barbara rushed off into the shadows, and Cassie dropped her weed and let out an annoyed sigh. "I can't go through this charade twice, Sly. I wish you'd just come up with some reason you can't make the wedding."

Sly walked to the edge of the pond and kicked a stone. The muscles in his jaw rippled as he watched the play of light across the surface. "I care about Barbara. She's like my own kid sister. I watched her grow up. I want to be there."

"Then maybe I shouldn't come."

Sly turned to her, his form silhouetted against the dim light of the moon's reflection on the water. Several feet separated them, but Cassie felt naked, transparent. "Our lives will always be intertwined in some way, Cass. We can't pretend they're not. We love the same people, and we have a stake in their lives. Neither one of us should have to cut off our roots just to avoid the other.''

"I'm not trying to avoid you.'' Cassie choked, the heat of conviction and confusion drying her throat. "We just can't pretend we're married indefinitely. It doesn't make sense.'' She thought of Sly's engagement, and the shock his marriage would be to the family. "We have to go on with our lives.'' She looked at the ground, where a heavier breeze was stirring the weeds at her feet. Blinking back the tears that were threatening her eyes, she sighed and turned away. "I'm going back to the house.''

His voice was barely audible over the wind and the sound of gravel under her shoes. "Don't go, Cass.''

Swallowing with great effort, she turned around. The breeze caught the fabric of her dress and lifted it in a swirl. Her hair whipped into her face, and she swept it back. "There's no point in standing out here with you, Sly,'' she said. "It's not getting us anywhere.''

"I don't want it to get us anywhere,'' he said softly. "I'm tired of rushing forward as if yesterday were after me. I only want to stand still for a minute, and share some innocent memories with my best friend. Is that so wrong?''

Cassie hugged her waist and closed her eyes, struggling with the incipient tears threatening to spill over her lashes. How could he have expressed in so simple a way the emotion that had stabbed at her all day?

His voice came closer now, and he pushed the hair out of her face, letting his fingers mold to the shape of her cheekbone. Stepping behind her, he slipped his arms around her waist, interweaving them with hers, and rested his head on her hair. "It's hard to come back here and not remember swimming in this pond with you, or riding bareback across the pasture, or greeting the sun when it came up over there after we made love for the first time." His voice was mesmerizing, comforting, and Cassie opened her eyes and saw the memories through a misty blur. "And it's especially hard to forget that this was the backdrop for our wedding. I won't erase it all, Cass. I can't just pretend that none of it ever happened. All of it made me what I am."

Biting her lip, Cassie closed her eyes again. "I know," she whispered.

His arms tightened around her waist, and he dipped his head to drop a kiss on her neck. His voice at her ear was deep and nostalgic. "Remember how we planned to build a house out there? We were going to build it ourselves. We didn't know what we'd do for a living, but we knew we'd be so good at it that we'd never have to leave home. Everyone would come to us." He breathed a voiceless laugh. "We were so enthusiastic. So full of life."

"We were dreamers," Cassie whispered.

"Maybe," he said. "But we didn't know it."

The night music filled the silence that fell between them, drawing them closer than the superficiality of words. After several moments, Sly spoke again. "I think losing those dreams was our biggest mistake."

Stiffening at the too painful probing, but yet unable to pull completely away, Cassie said, "We just grew up."

"Maybe so," he agreed in a duller voice, dropping his arms and breaking the contact between them. He rubbed his face wearily, a breath tearing from his lungs as he slid his hands into his pockets, looking heavenward. "But I sure could use a couple of dreams right about now."

Cassie, who knew in the deepest part of her the need he spoke of and the fact that it had nothing to do with his profession, cast his words off lightly in the hope of changing the subject. "You're doing better than we ever expected, Sly. You're very successful."

His laugh cut the night and Cassie's heart. "Yeah. I'm doing great. And so are you." Cassie wrenched her eyes from the sarcastic set of his face and the tight smile directed at her. "I guess when you let go of one dream, the rest die easy." His voice lowered as he kicked a rock into the water and watched it disappear. "Class President and Homecoming Queen. Achievers. Isn't that what you and I have always been?" A deep, exhausted breath issued from his lips. "And all that is as much bull as the fact that we still share a name."

His sudden shift in mood disarmed Cassie. "Sly, I—"

"Just drop it, Cass," he said, taking her arm and starting back toward the house. "Let's just get through the weekend the best we can. I'll try to keep my distance and refrain from reminiscing, if you'll try to hold your contempt for me down to a discreet level."

And before she could find a reply, he had dropped her arm and was steps ahead of her on the worn path home.

Chapter Three

Sly's expression changed from anger to subdued indifference when he and Cassie emerged from the darkness of the trees to the animated circle of the group. Cassie tried to slip inside the house to collect her thoughts and tame her emotions, but before she could make the escape, Sasha was calling her.

"I have a surprise for both of you," the old woman said in her raspy voice, hooking an arm through Cassie's while she gestured for Sly to join them.

"Another one?"

"The best one," she answered, taking Sly's hand and pulling them both into the house. "This one's upstairs, so you'll have to give me a hand."

When they'd made their way to the top of the stairs, she led them down the long hall and stopped in front of the closed door of the room they'd shared when they'd first married. With a trembling hand, Sasha turned the knob and opened the door. Smiling broadly, she led them in.

Cassie and Sly caught their breath in unison when they saw what Sasha had done. The room, fairly plain and practical before, was now decorated as if awaiting a bride and groom's wedding night. "It's the bedroom I always dreamed of for Jesse and me," Sasha said, watching the battling reactions on each of their faces. "So when I heard you were coming home, I—"

Cassie suddenly felt her blood rush to her feet. She sank to the side of the bed and avoided meeting Sly's eyes. "Sasha, it's so...so lovely. But we're only going to be here for the weekend. And we—"

"I know, I know." Sasha cut off Cassie's words with a wave of her hand. "But I wanted to give you some incentive to come home more often. Do you like it, Sly?"

With the little woman's question, Cassie raised pleading eyes to Sly. He was walking around the room, feeling the texture of the wallpaper, fingering the lace of the curtains that fell from the canopy and was tied back with brown bows. Cassie wondered if he would resent having his childhood bedroom tampered with and made so feminine. It was one more change in the home that he needed to be the same. He turned back to them and smiled, his eyes expressive with thought. "I like it," he said. Wetting his lips, he studied his grandmother fondly. "You've worked so hard on this. It means a lot to us, Grandma."

"Then you'll come home more often?"

Cassie couldn't stand much more, and closing her eyes, she lowered her head to her hand.

"Of course we will," Sly said.

Cassie snapped her head up, shooting him a narrow glance that spoke more potently than words. "Sasha," she said, standing up and going to the woman, ignoring Sly's laser looks. "We really do love all this, and you were so sweet to do it for us, but—"

"But it must have cost a fortune," Sly cut in, wrapping an arm around his grandmother's small shoulders. "We insist on paying you back."

"You will not!" Sasha said adamantly. "What else have I got to do with my money?"

Cassie glared at Sly for changing the subject before she could break the news of their hotel room, but before she could start again, he had turned Sasha around and was walking her out of the room. "Well, how about if we have your room done?"

"My room is just the way I like it!" Sasha snapped. "Don't you dare touch it."

Grinding her teeth in rage, Cassie watched them head for the stairs, and when Sly looked back at her, she narrowed her eyes and mouthed, "I want to talk to you."

Nodding, he turned back to his grandmother and helped her down the stairs.

Standing in the open doorway, Cassie turned back to the room and blew out a long breath. It would have been a dream years ago, she thought. She imagined Sly and herself as newlyweds, making love on the satin bedspread, enclosed by lace draped all around the bed, smelling the intoxicating fragrance of the freshly cut flowers she knew Sasha had picked and arranged herself. But now it was only a reminder of what once had been, what had never been meant to be.

Before she'd even heard his footsteps on the stairs, Sly was beside her, staring at the bed as he leaned against the jamb. His lack of comment made Cassie furious, so she went across the room to the window and turned to him. "Either you tell her or I will. This is getting out of hand."

Sly breathed a laugh and glanced up the hall as if making sure no one would hear. "Do you think I like this any more than you do?"

The amused sparkle in his eyes told her he did. "I didn't notice you making too many objections," she bit out.

Sly trained his eyes on the ceiling and shook his head. "Do you know how long that wonderful little woman down there had to work to get this room like this? Do you have any idea how hard it must have been for her to work with this lace and this satin?"

"I know, Sly," Cassie said implacably, "but it's all for a lie."

Sly closed the door and was in front of Cassie in four swift steps. "Then you go down there and tell her it's a lie," he said, his eyes taking on the challenging heat of his temper as he leaned toward her. "You go tell her that you appreciate all the hard work, but that we'd rather stay in a hotel. Then break her heart by telling her we've been divorced for a year. If you're cold enough to do that, be my guest."

Cassie covered her face and went to the bed. "Damn you, Sly Farrell! I knew I shouldn't have come here with you!"

Sly's gait was restrained and deliberate as he walked to the adjoining bathroom door and glanced in. Setting his elbow on the jamb, he scratched an eyebrow with his thumb. "Well, you did, Cass. And whether you like it or not, we're stuck together. I'm sorry it turned out this way. I really am. But I can sacrifice a little comfort and convenience for my grandmother. It won't kill either one of us."

"I don't want to break her heart," Cassie moaned. "All I want to do is go to the hotel suite and sleep alone in my own bed, in my own room. I should think you'd feel the same way, considering Amanda."

"This is between you and me, Cass," he bit out. "Amanda has nothing to do with it."

Cassie tugged at her hair. "Separate beds, Sly. Is that so much to ask?"

Sly slammed his hand against the casing, mouthing an expletive, then went to the door, shaking his head as he opened it. "Ask and find out," he offered with contempt. "I'll be downstairs. Do what you want."

Cassie sat in the room alone for a moment after he left her, studying the amount of privacy they could have from each other, mentally measuring the width of the bed, which seemed even narrower than the one they'd shared as husband and wife. "Damn!" she muttered again at her lack of alternatives, then hurried down the stairs.

Sly and Sasha were back on the patio talking with the others, and when Cassie walked out she met his impassive gaze that left her feeling strangely empty. She imagined how he saw her, how he would see her if she broke the illusion all of these people had of them. In spite of everything, she did not want him to see her as a villain. Taking a deep, resolute breath, Cassie went to Sasha, hugged her affectionately, kissed her cheek, and thanked her again for the room. Then she looked up at Sly and said, "Why don't you take the suitcases on up?"

His warm, grateful, tremendously relieved smile made the gesture worthwhile. Winking, he nodded and went for the luggage.

When Cassie's half of the family had gone home and most of Sly's had retired for the night, Cassie realized they were both delaying the inevitable. Stretching, she stood up and looked at Sly's father. "I'd better go on up if I'm going to get up in time for the picnic tomorrow. Don't want to have circles under my eyes at my class reunion." She hoped Sly would have the grace to stay behind until she was dressed and in bed, maybe even asleep, before he came up.

Unfortunately, Sly had other plans. "Yeah, we'd better go on up," he said, an incorrigible, challenging grin spreading over his face, which Cassie did her best to ignore.

Saying their good-nights, Sly escorted Cassie to their bedroom, a proprietary hand pressed against the small of her back. The room was lit in a yellow hue from the lamp, setting an atmosphere that Cassie wanted very much to dispel. Turning on the bright overhead light, she went in.

"Why don't you relax?" Sly asked quietly as he closed the door and watched her drag her luggage to her side of the room and open it. "Take a hot bath or something. You're making me nervous."

Cassie cocked her head and looked at him. "How am I making you nervous?"

"Your silence, for one thing. And you're all tense and guarded, like you're afraid I might attack you. I swear, I won't attack you." The half grin on his face infuriated her.

"I can take care of myself," she muttered, sifting roughly through her suitcase and tossing her clothes into the empty drawers.

Sly disappeared into the bathroom, and in a moment she heard the sound of running bathwater, and the air became laced with sweet-scented steam drifting across the room. When Sly came back into the bedroom, Cassie threw him a glance over her shoulder. "Aren't you going to smell a little feminine?"

"It's for you," he said "Sasha left some bubble bath."

An ominous rush of heat colored Cassie's face, and she stood up, her fists riding her hips. "I don't need a bubble bath. Just a regular hot bath will be fine."

Sly shrugged and snapped open his own suitcase. "Then let it out and fill it back up the way you want it."

Defeated, Cassie blew out a weary breath and stooped back down to her suitcase, deciding not to press the issue. She looked through her underwear for the long gown and robe she had packed, then remembered her lost suitcase. "Oh, no," she moaned. "I forgot to call about my suitcase. It had my gown in it." She looked at Sly, catching the grin sauntering across his face before he rubbed his jaw to cover it.

"You can wear one of my T-shirts," he offered, pulling one out and tossing it across the bed to her.

Knowing she had nothing better in her own suitcase, she took it and went into the bathroom. Already the mirror and chrome were fogged, and a cloud of steam drifted above the bubbles. Tying her hair up off her neck, she stepped out of her clothes and into the hot water. The tension literally melted from her muscles, and the fragrance of luxury wrapped her in relaxation.

When she'd finished her bath, she dried carefully and slipped into fresh underwear and the long T-shirt Sly had given her. With her damp hair still tied up, she came out of the bathroom.

Sly was lying on the bed, arms crossed behind his head, staring up at the ceiling. He had changed, too, and was now dressed only in a pair of blue shorts. His right leg was bent, the long muscles of his thigh flexing as his toes stroked the satin of the bedspread. Trying not to notice the hard curves of his biceps and the broad slashes of muscle across his chest, Cassie walked barefoot to the suitcase and dropped her clothes in. Self-consciously, she tugged at the T-shirt, making sure it at least covered her underwear, though she knew her thighs were completely exposed.

Turning back to the bed, she watched him roll onto his side to face her, his head propped on a hand in a centerfold pose. Wrenching her eyes away from him and crossing her arms guardedly, she focused on a spot on her pillowcase. "Couldn't you wear a little more than that?" she asked, annoyance clear in her voice.

Sly pulled up to a sitting position, a less-than-innocent smile glittering in his sapphire eyes. "This is what I sleep in."

"Just this once?" she pressed.

As if to accommodate her, Sly pulled himself off the bed. But instead of going to his suitcase to find something more to wear, he went around the bed to Cassie and hooked a hand over the canopy, cocking his head and grinning down at her. "Afraid you can't control yourself?" he asked, his eyes boring into her for a sign of the truth.

"Don't be ridiculous," she quipped. "I just don't think we should be so personal with each other."

That seductive grin broadened slowly across Sly's face, and he leaned toward her until their noses almost touched. In a deep rumble, he said, "Pretty lady, you should know better than to stand in nothing but bikini panties and your husband's T-shirt with your body responding right through the fabric, and talk about being too personal. Isn't 'intimate' more the word you're looking for?"

"You're not my husband," Cassie said, crossing her arms higher to cover the points that gave away her arousal.

His grin eased wider, baring his perfect white teeth, and he stepped closer, taking her shoulders as the crisp hair narrowing down his stomach brushed against her folded arms. "All right," he breathed. "I'll give you that one."

His eyes held hers imprisoned, and he slid his hand around her neck to the bow tying her hair. His grin faded slowly as her auburn hair dropped around her shoulders, and his serious, seductive appraisal made her abandon the fleeting notion to pull away. Against her arms she felt his abdominal muscles tighten with control. He swallowed visibly and wet his lips. All the energy and defense Cassie had stored for such an instance was transformed and concentrated in the desire coiling in the pit of her stomach. When his face began lowering to hers, his lips hovering for an eternity, offering her ample time to object before they pos-

sessed her, she was powerless to move away. Without
thought, she tilted her head and opened her moist lips
for him, accepting the familiar taste and the warm,
gentle, careful probing, as a long slow moan of relief
escaped his throat. His hands slid down her back and
pulled her against him, and her own dropped their
guard of her breasts and went to the smooth, soft flesh
of his waist and the taut, rounded muscles of his back.

The more Cassie offered, the more Sly demanded.
His kiss went from tasting to devouring as his own
arousal pressed hard and determined against her. One
hand slid to the scrap of cloth of her panties, arous-
ing currents of sensation with each circular movement, while the other brushed up under her shirt,
slowly coaxing his way to the breasts aching for the
feel of his calloused fingers. His mouth moved against
hers, the rhythm of his breath matching the thrust of
his lower body, as his fingers found the summits of her
breasts and drew need from her that could never be
sated.

The hand pressing her against his lower body slid
inside her panties, kneading the soft flesh there,
pressing her harder against him until she thought she
would die with need. His lips moved to her eyelids,
tasting every inch of her face, tickling her with his hot
breath and awakened passion, as one hard leg pushed
between her thighs. "I could never forget you, Cass,"
he whispered in a husky, quivering voice. "And I
tried. I really tried."

Without breaking the contact of their bodies, he
lifted her and lowered her to the bed, the change in
positions slowly bringing her to her senses. "We
can't," she breathed as he lowered his mouth to her

throat and slowly began to work her panties down over her hips. "No, we can't. It's not fair."

"Why?" he asked in a whisper while his hands continued pushing the wisp of nylon over the firm length of her thighs.

"It's a lie," she choked. "It's not real. It's just a fantasy. A memory." She reached for his hands to stop him from going further.

"Baby, it is real," he said, his eyes as smoky-blue as the first stage of dusk. Abandoning her disrobing, he slid up the length of her, the hard weight of his body pressing her into the mattress. "This is real."

"No," she said, rolling out from under him. The act was like denying herself a breath after being trapped underwater, but she forced herself to be strong. "It's not real. It hasn't been real for a year."

"This is the *most* real it's been for a year," he said, raising himself and gazing into her brilliant emerald eyes with pleading need.

"I can't deal with it," she said firmly, restoring order to her clothes and pulling herself off the bed onto legs suddenly weak with denial. "I'm sorry. I just can't deal with it right now."

And without looking back, she rushed into the bathroom and closed the door. The cold ceramic tile beneath her feet lent a feeling of reality to a day that had resembled something out of a bad dream. Leaning against the door, she slid down until she sat on the floor, crossing her legs and staring at a spot on the wall. *The most real it has been in a year,* she thought. For her, maybe. But not for him. Not for him.

Biting her lip, she fought with the memory of a vulnerable time a few months ago, when she had needed

Sly more than she ever had. When she had realized that she had been wrong to leave him. When she had admitted to herself that she had never stopped loving him. Her pulse sped with renewed anguish now as she recalled the careful way she had packed for her trip to Chicago to see him, how she had hoped to surprise him, how she had planned to fly back into his arms and take up where they had left off. But the surprise had been hers.

Cassie pressed the heels of her hands against her eyes as she remembered the arrival "home." She had used her key to get in, but before she had called his name, the atmosphere had stopped her. Soft music had been the first clue, followed by the two wineglasses on the coffee table and the half-empty bottle of Chablis. The table was decorated in candlelight and bore evidence of a gourmet meal that someone had obviously cooked for Sly—for she knew he was as inept in the kitchen as he was skilled in the bedroom.

A black high-heeled shoe caught her attention at the bottom of the stairs, and another lay on its side halfway up, as if it had fallen that way when the woman had been carried to bed.

Feeling foolish for having believed that things could be resumed, Cassie had quietly backed out of the house and driven her rental car back to the airport, and Sly had never known she had been there. She felt betrayed, even though her intellect told her she had no hold on a man she had divorced. Had she thought he'd be pining away for her all that time? Had she believed he'd be waiting for her?

From that moment on she had decided that their relationship was over for good. Frank had brought her stories of Sly's many romances and she had convinced herself that she didn't care. But it had been a harder blow, she realized now, to learn that he had settled down to one woman—the woman who would take her place once and for all.

Harsh reality had kept her from harboring illusions about Sly. She knew where she stood with him.

So how had he managed to make her melt in his arms the first night they were back together?

Cassie stood up and leaned over the sink, ran some water, and splashed it into her face. At least they had gotten it out of the way, and now she had made it clear that she couldn't go through with making love to him again. Too many ties still bound them together. Too many ties that could strangle them when they each went their separate ways again.

Taking a deep breath, Cassie opened the door and saw that Sly had turned off the light. He was in bed again, the satin covers pulled to his waist, and his eyes were closed. Without saying a word, she went to her side of the bed and slipped between the sheets.

After several moments of silence, Sly spoke. "Maybe one of us should sleep in a chair or something," he said quietly.

She swallowed and covered her forehead with the back of her wrist. "Maybe."

Another silence followed, until Sly said in a louder voice, "That would be pretty stupid. We slept together for eleven years without any catastrophes."

"Then why did you bring it up?" she asked, her eyes fixed on the ceiling.

"I knew you were thinking it."

Not able to deny that, Cassie didn't answer. Silence filled the room like a heavy fog, cut only by the sound of their breathing. Glancing from the corner of her eye, she saw that Sly's eyes were open, his black lashes curled against the moonlit square of light reflecting off the wall. His jaw rippled, and his arms, bent and clasped behind his head, bulged with muscles that seemed more powerful than ever.

His broad chest heaved with a deep sigh that seemed to rip out of him, and without looking at her, he said, "Cass, I know it's an ordeal for you, but I'm really glad to have you here with me this weekend. I've missed you."

Cassie couldn't answer, for the raw statement was so unexpected, so naked, that it left her stunned. But the tragedy of the confession cut into her heart, for she knew it wasn't enough. She missed him, too, but that would never be enough. Swallowing, she touched his tense biceps, and he covered her hand, rolling his head to look at her. Their eyes locked and embraced for a fraction of a moment before Sly looked away.

When Cassie pulled her hand back, Sly whispered, "Good night," and turned his back to her.

A torturing memory tugged at her heart, a memory of his curling up in the bend of her body while they slept, his hand pressed against the full abdomen that had carried their child. Turning away from him, she curled into herself, arms around her waist, and fought the tears of latent grief and aching regret.

The tears did not come, and neither did sleep for a while. But the rhythmic sound of his breathing lulled her into a restless state of semiconsciousness full of memories and dreams that she had no energy to separate.

When sleep finally caught her and coaxed her under its spell, she slept as soundly as when she had been Sly's bride. So when she awoke the following morning to find herself trapped in the curve of his powerful arm, the palm of his hand pressed against her bare rib cage, their legs entangled, and her head resting on the crisp, curling hair of his chest, she thought for a moment of drowning herself in the bathtub.

But that was impossible, for when she tried to slip out of his hold without waking him, his arms only tightened, and a faint, slow grin gave infuriating life to his otherwise dormant features.

Chapter Four

Y ou've got a lot of nerve," Cassie mumbled, jerking out of Sly's grasp and sliding to the opposite edge of the bed.

Sly's chest quaked with quiet laughter, and he peered at her through the narrow half-moons of his eyes. "Me? What did I do?"

Cassie pushed the tangled strands of hair out of her face and stood up. "I don't want to discuss it."

Pursing his lips to fight his grin, he propped himself on an elbow and shrugged. "All right. Guess you just woke up on the wrong side of the bed."

Cassie snatched her pillow off the bed and held it in front of her to hide her full breasts under Sly's T-shirt. "You better believe I woke up on the wrong side of the bed! *Your* side, you—"

"Wait a minute!" Sly said, sitting up and reaching for her shoulders. "Before you go accusing me of something that wasn't my fault, you'd better get your facts straight.''

Cassie shook off his hands and stormed around the bed to the bathroom door. "I don't think your facts coincide with mine, Sly," she said, going in and slamming the door behind her.

Turning on the water, she leaned over the sink and splashed a cold handful in her face. A heavy thump sounded on the door, and she knew Sly was leaning against it.

"You're crazy, you know that?" he asked through the barrier.

"I can't hear you," she said. "The water's running."

"Then turn it off!"

A moment passed while Cassie brushed her teeth, desperately trying to ignore the fact that he was still waiting at the door, mentally stomping out the feelings that had overcome her when she'd awakened in Sly's arms. *Damn him!*

"Turn off the water, Cass," Sly said in a dull, controlled voice from the other side of the door. "If I raise my voice the whole house will hear us."

Cassie left the water running and leaned against the sink, mentally berating herself for being an idiot. Hadn't she known that coming home with Sly would ruin her? Hadn't she known that her resistance would only awaken the innate competitiveness he'd grown up with? She was a woman, an attractive one. And he was a man who had spent much of the past year being Chicago's most available bachelor. What hurt was not that he had exposed her vulnerability, but that it didn't matter to him. She was just another playmate. Another challenge. She wondered if he often stepped out on Amanda.

The door thudded open and Cassie jumped as Sly came in, his face taut with conflicting emotions. "Get out of here!" She clipped the words, stepping back. "If you can't give me privacy in my sleep, you can at least have the decency to leave me alone in the bathroom."

"Cass, I didn't do anything. You came to *me* last night. You were asleep and you just—"

Cassie turned her back to Sly and clenched her fists. "So you took advantage of it!"

"All I did was hold you," he said in a broken voice.

"You shouldn't have," she said, forcing the emotion from her face and turning back to him. "You had no business—"

"You're my wife," he said with slow emphasis.

"I'm not your wife!" she flung back. "I'm a part of your past and that's all. There is nothing between us anymore. Nothing!"

He stood there for a moment, the weight of his upper body poised against the door, staring at her as if the mere act would crumble her defenses and the barrier she had constructed between them. Silence rang a deafening peal, like an alarm that warned of destruction. Was there more to say? Would there ever be more they could say? She saw his Adam's apple bob, but he offered no other clues to his thoughts. Finally, without cutting the tension, he stepped from the bathroom and closed the door.

Pain greater than humiliation or loneliness coursed through her, an inexplicable grief that flushed her veins at times when she was least equipped to deal with it. Sweeping her hands through tangled hair, she squeezed her eyes shut and reminded herself how strong she was, how strong she had become in the past few months. She had survived these stirrings before, and she would get through them now. All she had to do was not feel, not think. All she had to do was focus on something else.

Hurrying out of the bathroom, she grabbed a pair of shorts and a shirt and went back in to put them on, never making eye contact with the man who lay prone on the bed, staring at the ceiling. When she came out, she went to the bed table for her hairbrush, but Sly caught her hand before she could pull away. Sitting up on the bed, he gazed into her eyes. "I'm sorry I upset you, Cass," he said in a voice that soothed and grieved her at the same time. "I didn't mean to."

"I'm okay," she said hurriedly. "I never have been easy to get along with before my first cup of coffee." The admission was the closest she could come to an apology for her harsh words. More than that would be wrought with tenderness that might expose all the regret she had tried so hard to hide. "I'm going down to see if there's any coffee perking."

She disengaged her hand, but his hovered in the air for a moment before closing and dropping in a fist on the mattress. "I'll see you downstairs," she muttered, then left the room.

The pungent smell of freshly brewed coffee lent a welcome sense of reality to the weekend. Pushing through the swinging kitchen door, Cassie saw Sasha, clothed in a thick robe that made her tiny frame look even more fragile, standing before the oven, peering through the window at the homemade biscuits that were rising to a golden brown.

"Smells wonderful," Cassie said when the old woman saw her.

"Come in here and sit down," Sasha said with her shoulders raised in excitement. "You can have first pick. Pour yourself some coffee and I'll get the jam." Sasha's eyes followed Cassie as she poured her coffee, then sat down at the long table. "I was just thinking of fixing you and Sly a box of my preserves and some of the vegetables I've put up. Do you think it would keep on the plane? Do you think you'd eat it? You two are so busy with your jobs I don't know how you manage to eat anything decent. When do you cook? 'Course, by now I suppose you've trained Sly to fend for himself, huh?" A hoarse laugh followed. "If you did, honey, you've worked a miracle I never managed."

Cassie smiled at the one-sided conversation Sasha was delighting in. "He does okay." Knowing there was no need to say more to encourage Sasha's ramblings, she sipped at her coffee and glanced hungrily toward the oven.

"Be patient," Sasha said with a wave of her hand. "They'll be ready in a minute." She took Cassie's free hand in both her own and patted it. "Now, tell me all about your job. I never hear much about you. How much traveling do you do? Isn't your home office in New York? How do you manage to keep things going from Chicago?"

Cassie took another sip while she sorted out her stories, knowing Sasha would notice immediately if her version didn't match Sly's. "I travel a lot," she said cautiously. "I spend a lot of time at the New York store, but it isn't necessary for me to have an office there." That was true enough, she thought, since she'd kept her office at the Chicago store as long as she and Sly were married. Not certain how much Sasha did know about her work, she glanced at the biscuits again, hoping to distract her from the subject.

"Oh, all right. They're probably ready by now, anyway," Sasha said on a laugh. Taking the hot pan from the oven, she turned back to Cassie. "Times have changed, though," she said, as if adding to a thought she'd just interrupted. "For the better, I think, too. Women can do all the things you do and not feel guilty. Sly's grandpa, understanding man that he was, would have hog-tied me if he'd ever thought I wanted to launch out and do anything on my own."

Cassie laughed. "Come on, Sasha. You've always been the most independent woman I know. I can't imagine you being subject to any man's orders."

Sasha winked and leaned over the table, her voice reverently low. "I'm not saying I didn't do anything on my own. I'm just saying that I had sense enough always to make him think it was his idea. Women had to be more subtle back then. We had to distract our men with other things. My mama was Greek, you know. She had some tricks to pass on that you wouldn't believe, and I used them all."

"I can imagine," Cassie giggled. "I'll bet you were some kind of lady."

"No different than you, honey," she said, knifing the biscuits off the pan and setting them on a plate for Cassie.

"Yes, you are. You're a lot stronger than I am."

Sasha set the plate in front of Cassie and opened a jar of strawberry jam. "Cassie, I'd be willing to bet there's strength in you that you've never even tapped," she said as she lowered her small frame into the chair across from Cassie. "Maybe you just haven't needed to call on it yet. Or maybe you use it for the wrong things. Strength can be a very lonely thing if it's used wrongly."

Cassie's eyes locked with Sasha's, still alert and alive though her body seemed so frail. Was she so transparent, Cassie wondered, that people could see in her what she could not see herself?

"I'll tell you about strength," Sasha went on with a twinkle in her clear eyes. "I remember a little eight-year-old girl whose dog got hit by a truck. Little rascal lifted her chin, marched right out into that street, and picked up that lifeless little animal. Buried him herself, and never shed a tear. At least not in front of anyone—"

Amazement and warmth stirred inside Cassie. "You remember that?"

Sasha smiled and patted her hand, her head moving in its perpetual tremor. "It's one of my earliest memories of you. I thought, 'That little thing is going to go far.' Just wish it didn't have to be clear across the country." She laughed again, deepening the lines that mapped her face, lines that created the wonderful expression so unique to Sasha.

"What's so funny?" Sly asked from the doorway.

Cassie's smile faded, and she glanced at Sly. He leaned against the jamb holding the swinging door open, his shower dampened hair mussed as if it had been towel-dried and never brushed. He wore noth-

ing but a pair of cut-off jeans, and he held his sneak-
ers by two hooked fingers. In the morning light filling
the kitchen through the windows, Cassie noted the
tanned highlights of his skin and the brown circles of
his nipples. The dark down of hair curling on his chest
branched into a *T* and tapered down his hard stomach to disappear behind his zipper. Wrenching her eyes
away, she took a final gulp of her coffee.

"We were just reminiscing," Sasha said, patting the
seat next to her for him to take.

"Am I interrupting?" he asked Cassie, his eyes
making the slightest contact with hers before darting
away.

"Not at all," Cassie answered as politely as possible.

Sasha stood up and poured Sly a cup of coffee, then
refilled Cassie's cup. "You have no idea how happy I
am to have you two here."

"We're happy to be here, Grandma."

"You know I remember exactly when you two fell
in love? Bet you don't even remember, do you?"

"Well, uh—"

"You were fourteen, Sly, and it was right before
Cassie's fourteenth birthday. Up till then you'd been
best friends, wrestling all the time like little boys,
playing tricks on each other. I remember you found
her a pearl barrette for her hair, and you wrapped it up
to give it to her for her birthday."

The memory came back from dusty corners of
Cassie's mind, setting her heart fluttering as if it had
happened today. He had taken her into the barn and
asked if he could give her that present early, because
he didn't want her opening it in front of everyone else.

She remembered the tremor in her fingers as she'd untied the bow and carefully torn the paper off, and the way he fidgeted while he awaited her expression. Her heart had threatened to fly out of her chest like a captured bird, and when she opened the box...

"Cassie, you came out of that barn with that barrette in your hair, and Sly was following you with the proudest smile on his face I ever saw."

She had looked up into his eyes and thanked him, feeling the pink blush of alien feeling on her cheeks, reflecting the way his neck reddened and the strange quiver of his lips when he shrugged and tried to smile. He had kissed her then, a soft, innocent kiss that came as a complete surprise to them both. Neither had known what to do after that threshold had been crossed. She had felt so inept. So awkward. So wonderful.

"After that you never touched each other for weeks, and you had trouble looking each other in the eye," Sasha said with a sparkling of her dark eyes as she settled down again. "For weeks Sly was a holy terror to live with. Moody, temperamental. And you two went out of your way to keep from being alone with each other, but when others were around it was blatantly obvious that all you wanted *was* to be alone with each other." Sasha sighed. "I knew right then you had fallen in love."

Cassie glanced across the table at Sly and saw that he was caught in his own memories. A warm, faint smile lit his face as he stared nostalgically into his coffee. Under the table, his bare foot brushed her ankle and moved back, and their eyes made momentary contact again.

"We had no idea anyone else knew, Grandma," Sly said, smiling a wistful, secretive smile at Cassie, as if they alone knew the extent of the emotions they had cultivated in each other. The smile was more than Cassie could bear. The lie was more than she could stand. Her eyes tore from his and found a chip in the fingernail polish she'd slapped on so haphazardly the day before.

"It couldn't have been more obvious," the old woman said, but the joy of memory was gone from her voice, and a dull monotone colored it now. Cassie looked up and saw that the smile had faded from Sasha's face, too, and her eyes were sad and focused on a spot on the table.

Before Cassie could think of a change of subject or analyze the sudden shift in Sasha's mood, Sly's brother burst through the door.

"Are you people crazy?" Sammy asked without a word of greeting. "I thought I was the only one around here who got up at dawn." He went to his grandmother, whose eyes regained their life, and kissed her on the cheek. "What's for breakfast, Grandma?"

The room came to life as each family member awoke and joined them at the table. Cassie helped cook breakfast, trying to ignore the heaviness weighing on her heart. Conversation at the table, though perfectly natural to everyone else, seemed stiff and stilted to Cassie. Inevitably the subject continued to drift around to herself and Sly, and the quick way Sly answered all the questions so that it would have convinced even her that they were still as happy as ever, made her angry.

The clatter of dishes being put away and happy family voices chattering about irrelevant things finally lightened Cassie's spirits. She busied herself loading the dishwasher, hoping the activity would keep her from having to participate in any more lies concerning her and Sly. But no sooner had the last plate been cleared from the table, than Sly's father called her to follow him outside.

"Don't try to get out of it," he told Sly who was waiting outside for her. "We haven't had pictures of you two in about five years. Just grin and bear it."

Cassie didn't know how much more she could take. "Jasper, I can't. Really. I look awful, and I need to get ready for the picnic...."

"You look fine," Jasper declared. "I don't plan to send this in to *Cosmopolitan*, anyway. Just a few shots of my firstborn and his bride."

Breathing back her frustration, Cassie put her hands in her pockets and went to stand beside Sly, who was studying the gravel at his feet. "I don't want to do this, Sly," Cassie whispered.

"I know you don't," he said, turning to look over her shoulder so his father couldn't hear his words. "But it's important to him. Besides, we don't have any pictures together."

Gritting her teeth, she whispered, "We don't *need* any pictures together."

Sly set his eyes on something far beyond the pasture spread behind them like a studio backdrop. "Cass, I don't think it'll kill you to pretend you like me for a few minutes. I'm sorry if I'm cramping your style this weekend, but we didn't part enemies, if I remember right." He glanced back at his father, who had decided his film was tangled inside the camera and was busy pulling it back out. "If you want to know the truth, I'm not quite sure what you'd call that friendly, mature way we separated. But if that wasn't a farce I don't understand why this is."

Cassie struggled to swallow the lump that was blocking her throat, but she turned her back to Jasper. "How would you have preferred it? It was what we both wanted."

"Yeah," Sly said on a dull laugh. "No reason for any fireworks, right? Just a signature, a quick trip to Mexico, and a good-bye."

"Did you want fireworks?"

Sly laughed again and glanced after his father, who had disappeared into the house for another camera. "It might have helped. God knows there were moments when I wanted to scream at you. But when that wall goes up no one can get to you."

Cassie bit her lip and kicked at a rock. "Right. It was all my fault."

"I didn't say that, Cass," he said. "It's just that I've never been able to figure out where either of us went wrong."

"Maybe you shouldn't dwell on it," she said quietly. "Maybe you should just put it behind you and not think about it."

"Like you do?"

Cassie's eyes darted up, and she saw the anxiety that was etched between his brows and webbing the corners of his eyes. She didn't answer, for she knew she had been unsuccessful at doing that herself. She had tried. God knew, she had tried.

Sly's eyes sparkled with moisture and he swallowed and squinted into the sun. "I can't do that, Cass. It doesn't work as well for me."

The screen door slammed before Cassie was pressed to respond, and Jasper came out with a new camera. "Come on, you two. You can do better than that. You look like a couple of strangers."

Sly set his arm on her shoulders and pulled her closer to him. Awkwardly, stiffly, they stood smiling at the camera.

"If you think I plan to waste my film on a shot like that, you're sadly mistaken," Jasper said with exasperation.

Sly looked down at Cassie, dread in his eyes. "Sorry, Cass," he whispered. Cassie forced a smile and looked through the door as some of the others came outside to watch. At the kitchen window stood Sasha, watching with an expressionless gaze.

"Sasha's watching," Cassie said, sliding her arms around Sly's waist and leaning her head against his chest. Sly's arms folded around her, and he pulled her more tightly against him. The camera snapped.

"More, more!" Sammy chided from the steps. "Let's see some action!"

"How about a kiss?" Jasper shouted, camera to his eye.

"Sure, Dad," Sly teased, letting Cassie go and starting for his father.

"Not me, you big idiot, *her*!"

Laughing, Sly went back to Cassie and leaned down to drop a kiss on her lips.

"Is that the best you can do?" Sammy teased. "If it is, maybe I should try. She's probably ready for a real man by now, anyway."

A challenging half grin lightened Sly's features, and he turned to Cassie, pulled her theatrically against him, and kissed her. At first she resisted, embarrassed by their audience, but his arms only circled more firmly around her. Coaxing her lips open, he invaded the warmth of her mouth, his tongue laced with fire, waking senses that had been raw since he'd aroused them the night before. His head moved as the pressure grew, and her hands climbed his chest to brush across the unshaven roughness of his jaw, and through the midnight silk of his hair. From a distance, as if in another dimension, she heard cheers and laughter and applause. The masculine scent of his soap intoxicated her, and she wanted more, but knew she would never let herself indulge. His lips swept off hers and trailed to the corner of her mouth before he lifted his head.

"Way to go!" Sammy hooted above the others. "Dad got three shots out of that!"

His arms loosened, but he didn't let her go. Reluctantly, she dropped her hands and slid them back into her pockets, trying to grin as if the scene had cost her nothing. Sly gave a slight bow, smiling like an actor who'd just gotten a standing ovation. "That wasn't so bad, was it?" he asked Cassie in a husky whisper against her head.

"How much longer do we have to do this?" she asked, for she knew any admission of enjoyment at all would do her in.

"Good ol' Cass," he mumbled perceptively. "Always did love a good time."

Before she could defend herself, he slung an arm under her legs and lifted her with little effort. She gasped as his face burrowed into her stomach, and a ticklish scream gurgled from her throat as the camera snapped again. "Let go of me!" she shrieked between giggles. "When I get down from here I'm going to—Let go of me!" Her face was pink with the struggle as he bit her ribs and her waist and the most ticklish places that he had always used to make her putty. When she was defenseless, he set her down in front of him and wrapped his arms around her middle, resting his chin on her shoulder.

"One more, Dad, now that she's loosened up. Then we've got to go get ready for the reunion."

Cassie gave an authentic smile, crossed her arms over Sly's, and leaned back into him as the camera snapped. Then, as if she'd never found herself in his arms before, she stiffened and stepped away. His hands slid from her waist to her hips, and he pulled her back and dropped a kiss into the back of her hair as the group broke up and began to disperse. His arms tightened around her again, and he pulled her hips harder against him, communicating the intensity of his desire. His breath came heavy against her ear. "You did good, Cass."

His pulse beat into her back, racing against her own, and suddenly she didn't know if she could stand going up to that room alone with him. Worse, she thought, she didn't know if she could stand *not* going up to that room alone with him. The thought made her angry. "Don't you think we overdid it a little?" she asked in a cool voice as she slipped away from him, her rigid body warning him off.

"Just gave them what they wanted."

He always did, she thought. "I have to go in and get ready now," she said, leaving him standing alone as she went into the house.

The bathroom adjoining their bedroom was damp with the steam from Sly's shower, and his scent lingered in the air and drifted into the bedroom. A damp towel hung over the shower bar, and of its own accord, Cassie's hand went up to touch it. The familiarity of the sensations guiding her was frightening. She had forced herself to put him out of her mind for a year, clinging to the hurt and the bitterness as if they could save her from memory. But it was always a familiar moment like this that ambushed her. It came in different forms. One day a half ticket in an old purse that reminded her of a play they'd seen together. Another day it would be an old song. More often it presented itself as a need. She would be lonely. She would be down. And in the depths of her heart she would feel as if she'd thrown away life itself. With every fiber of her being, she would miss Sly.

Yet now she was with him, and she knew that all she had to do was go downstairs and approach him and he would be hers while they shared this weekend. But the divorce would still be a barrier between them, and so would his love for Amanda, and so would the things he had done and those she had not done when their marriage was breathing its last breaths. The baby would not come back just because they reunited, and the pain would not be lessened simply because he held her again. It would hurt more, for it would be like robbing the tragic event of its significance. They could never feel the same about their loss. She would never forget, and he would never know the same grief she knew.

Mechanically, Cassie applied her makeup and dressed in a bright yellow eyelet blouse that she tucked into her white shorts. It had always been Sly's favorite color on her, but that wasn't why she had worn it, she told herself. She wanted to look her best for her old friends. She didn't want them to have any indication that the homecoming queen and the class president had been less than successful in life. She didn't want them to know she had failed at the only things that had ever been important to her—marriage and motherhood.

A light knock sounded on the door, startling her from her reverie, and Sly stepped in. His expression was guarded; his eyes were hooded. "Are you finished with the bathroom?" he asked. "I need to shave."

She nodded. "Go ahead. I'm almost ready."

She watched as he went into the bathroom and turned on the water. From her position in a corner chair, she could smell the lathered shaving lotion as he spread it over his jaws. When he lifted his chin to take the first stroke with his razor, she lifted hers, too. As he turned his head, she turned hers, mesmerized by the slow, smooth strokes that would leave his skin soft to the touch until the stubble rose again in just a few hours. Wetting her lips, she studied the play of the muscles across his back as he leaned toward the mirror. When he was done, he rinsed the razor, splashed water on his face to rid it of the residual foam, and buried his face in a towel. Cassie turned away and concentrated on putting up her hair.

Sly came out of the bathroom and she heard his suitcase opening. A zipper sounded and the rustle of cloth sliding down his legs accelerated her breathing. Her heart pattered out a furious, uneven rhythm, and her hands trembled. A bobby pin fell from her fingers, but instead of turning around to pick it up, she took another and tried again. Again she heard the sound of rustling cloth, and another zipper. Why couldn't he change clothes in the bathroom? her mind cried. Didn't the man have any sense of . . . ?

His calloused hands closed around her trembling fingers, and he took the pin away from her. "Don't," he said in the softest voice she'd ever heard. "Just wear your hair down."

"But it'll be hot, and—"

His fingers began working the pins out of her hair. "I like it down."

The soft statement made it final, and Cassie made no objection as he pulled it from its twist, took the brush off the table, and brushed it around her shoulders. "Has it gotten darker since I saw you last?" he asked.

"Not that I know of," she answered in a hoarse, tremulous voice. "Is it redder?"

"Browner, I think," he said. He set the brush down and pushed out a long, heavy breath, then went back to his suitcase.

Silence was a burden that Cassie felt too weak to carry. But the alternative was more crushing. Slipping on her sandals, she found herself with nothing more to do. She looked at him as he tucked his shirt into his pants. His eyes were on her as if he had something to say but struggled with the words.

"There should be a lot of people there today," he said finally. "I'll be busy, since I'll be helping with the awards. I won't bother you."

"You don't bother me," she said helplessly.

"I make you uncomfortable," he said. "Maybe I try to sometimes. But I'll leave you alone today. No one will notice since everyone'll be playing catch-up anyway. Maybe that way you can relax a little."

The thought of their having to avoid each other gave Cassie a deep, sinking feeling. She was nervous about facing these people, nervous about having to uphold the lie, nervous about what their friends might have heard about her and Sly over the years. They were *their* crowd, *their* friends. Not just hers. It would be unnatural to be with them without Sly at her side. The realization that she had wanted to come home with him for that reason, among all the others, was disheartening. "And you can relax, too," she offered as she stood to get her purse.

"Yeah" was all he said as he followed her out of the room.

Chapter Five

The morning sun was climbing the arc of the sky to shine above the pine trees that skirted Langston Park when Sly pulled his father's car into the parking lot. "It's already hot," he said, glancing at Cassie.

Cassie didn't hear, for her attention was riveted on the throng of people scattered around the nucleus of picnic tables. A moment of panic gripped her, and she took a shivery breath and swallowed.

"You okay?"

Cassie tried to smile. How many more times would he ask her that, and in asking offer himself as her crutch? "I'm fine," she said, then with a laugh added, "just a little nervous."

Sly's cobalt gaze swept across the groomed lawn, through the playground equipment covered with children.

"What if I don't recognize anybody?" Cassie muttered.

Sly laughed. "Cass, we grew up with these people. No one could have changed that much. *We* haven't."

"Yes, we have."

Sly reached for the door handle, but when Cassie made no move to get out, he stopped. Her eyes were on the children waiting in line for the sliding board.

"They've all got kids," Sly said, almost as if the fact surprised him. "I didn't expect any of them to be that old. But I guess some of them could be in their teens if their parents married right after high school." A moment of quiet settled between them, a moment during which Cassie wondered what brand of insanity had made her come here to face her life. What was the use in moving to New York, leaving Sly, forgetting everything, when she had willingly come back here to have it all flung in her face?

"Are you sure you're okay, Cass?" Sly asked again. Cassie looked coldly at him, wondering how he could see their friends' children, anticipate all the questions and remarks about why they'd had none, and not feel as dreadful as she.

Shrugging, she opened the car door. "Let's just go on and get this over with," she said.

His hand came across the seat and settled on hers. "Hey, I thought you'd been looking forward to it."

"I don't feel the way I thought I would," she said, struggling with the emotions that were battling for a forum.

"You'll feel differently in a few minutes," Sly assured. "If not, I'll take you home."

Cassie nodded, got out, and met him at the front of the car where he folded her against him, his arms protectively around her for the long walk to the tables.

"Look at those people," he whispered playfully into her ear. "We must be the two best-looking ones here."

"He said modestly," Cassie commented with a grin.

"I mean it," he mumbled, and she knew the conspiratory teasing was meant to loosen her up, the same way the tickling had done that morning. Growling into her ear, he said, "Lady, you've got the best-looking legs within sixty miles of here."

"Thank you, Sly," she said, smiling easily up at him.

"Best-looking smile, too," he said, his blue eyes sparkling as they reached the crowd. "I'll hold to my promise, though. I'll leave you alone while we're here."

No sooner had the words been spoken than several old friends spotted them, pulling them apart with emotional handshakes and friendly embraces.

"Cassie Farrell, you come here!" a voice shrieked above the others. Cassie turned to see her oldest friend, Blair Callahue, cutting through the crowd. "Good grief, woman," the sleek blonde shouted, "didn't anyone tell you you're supposed to age in fifteen years?"

"Blair!" Cassie threw her arms around her, thankful that she seemed unchanged, as well. "I didn't think you'd come. Living on the west coast and all . . ."

"You thought I'd miss it?" She leaned toward Cassie, keeping her voice low. "It's a regular Peyton Place around here. Sally Andrews has *five* children! And Keith Picket is married for the third time. Let's see," she said, closing her eyes and making a mock mental calculation. "That's one for every five years. Sounds about right, considering the man. Anyway, his second wife remarried, too—Jerry Britton—remember the guy who used to win all the math awards? Glasses, brown hair?—so they're all here. Their kids are all mixed up and I can't tell you who goes with whom or if they belong to both of them. Bet you don't recognize that guy over there."

Beginning to relax and feel right at home beside Blair, Cassie stole a glance at the tall, handsome man her friend was pointing out. "I don't know him. Who is he?"

Blair grabbed Cassie by the arm and ushered her to a picnic table. "Sit down for this. You won't believe me. Remember Timothy Miller? The toothpick of a guy with oily hair and pimples? The one who always seemed to have a cast on one part of his body or another?"

"That's not him!" Cassie argued. "It couldn't be."

Blair nodded and exhaled a dreamy sigh. "It's him. Talk about outgrowing your weaknesses. I didn't believe it myself. Why couldn't any of us see that kind of potential in him back then?"

Cassie laughed. Blair had been divorced from a California entertainment attorney for four years, and her letters always related her hilarious experiences with men. Cassie wished she had taken divorce as well as her friend.

"I can't believe the changes," Blair was saying as she made a visual sweep of the crowd. "Oh, my God. Is that gorgeous creature over there Sly? I never thought the high-school heartthrob could actually get better looking, but—"

"Don't be melodramatic," Cassie cut in on a laugh, watching Sly herself.

"Melodramatic?" Blair repeated. "I'd stay close to him if I were you. There are divorced women lurking around just waiting to renew old friendships, and you're looking at one of them."

"What's this about divorced women?" a man asked from behind them.

Cassie turned around and saw one of the few men other than Sly she had ever dated in high school. "D.H.!" She gave him a quick hug, then pulled back to look at him. "You look great!"

"*You* look great," he said. "I've been watching you since you got here. Hi, Blair." Hugging her, too, he leaned a hip against the picnic table. "The two sexiest girls in the class."

"I didn't pay him to say that, Cassie. Did you?" Blair teased.

"The eyes are always the first to go," Cassie explained, grinning at D.H. "Where's all that hair you used to strut around here with? I thought they'd have to take your arms and legs before you'd surrender the hair."

D.H. laughed. "When I realized I'd have to get a job in order to support some of my habits, eating among them, I decided I'd have to conform. But deep in my heart I'm still a 'long-hair.' Speaking of hair," he said, leaning toward Cassie and lifting a silky auburn strand of hers, "why didn't you wear your hair long like this back then? If you had, I might not have been such a gentleman where Sly was concerned."

"What do you mean?" Cassie laughed. "You were no gentleman."

"I mean that I would have tried harder to steal you away from him."

Blair crossed her arms and cocked her head. "If I remember, you gave it a pretty good shot."

"Lost out, anyway," D.H. said with a shrug. Glancing across the crowd, he saw Sly watching their exchange and offered a sardonic wave, to which Sly did not respond.

"Uh, excuse me," D.H. said with a laugh. "But I think once again I'm on the wrong turf. I'll see you two later."

Cassie followed D.H.'s gaze and caught Sly's cool eyes as the man sauntered away. When Sly saw her watching, he turned back to the man he was talking with.

"Did I tell you about Katie Carson?" Blair asked, drawing Cassie's attention away. Smoothing back a fallen strand of hair and tucking it into her platinum chignon, Blair launched into a brief history of the ex-cheerleader while she sampled the food. Cassie avoided making eye contact with anyone else she didn't immediately recognize, for it was too difficult to tell who was a classmate and who was a spouse, and those she did recognize seemed so different that she wasn't sure she knew what to say. Taking refuge in Blair's babble, she leaned against the table. "Did you bring Staci?" she asked, searching the children on the playground for a miniature version of Blair.

"Over there. The one hanging upside-down on the monkey bars. If she'd had her way you would have been able to distinguish her by the punk-purple streaks in her hair, but I told her that was out of the question today. Little monster.''

Cassie shook her head and grinned. ''Blair, you're so maternal.''

Blair shrugged. ''What can I say? For eight years I've been doing battle with a little Cindy Lauper.'' She studied Cassie for a moment, and her smile faded. In a quiet voice, she said, ''Speaking of being maternal, Cassie, I've been wondering how you are. I haven't heard from you since you lost the baby.''

Cassie studied her damp palms, feeling a twinge of guilt for not answering Blair's concerned letters. She couldn't deal with the questions, and she had no intention of sharing the divorce with her. There had seemed no point in writing an evasive, meaningless letter, so she'd let it go. Lifting her chin, she scanned the faces until she came to Sly's again. He was watching her through the crowd, although he continued to chat with the classmates around him. ''I've been fine,'' Cassie heard herself say in a distant voice. ''Just real busy.'' She looked back at Blair, who was squinting her eyes against the sun behind Cassie's head. ''Listen, I'd appreciate it if you wouldn't mention any of that to anyone. I'm not up to long explanations, you know?''

''Of course,'' Blair said, turning toward the crowd, as if the delicate subject was closed. ''Well, you ready to dive in and mingle?''

Cassie grabbed Blair's arm when she started to stand. ''No. I can't mingle. I've got a terrible feeling that I'm at the wrong reunion. I've never seen these people before in my life.''

Blair laughed. "It just comes from living in another state. You get used to a whole different set of faces."

"But you seem to be doing okay."

"Give yourself an hour and you'll feel like you never left. I studied the yearbook last night, but the hard part is trying to reconstruct."

"Reconstruct?"

"Yeah, you know. Add hair to the men, take pounds off the women—very few of these people still resemble their pictures in the yearbook. The guys all cut their hair and quit wearing Nehru jackets. Can you believe it? My hair is actually *longer* than Jack Trait's now."

Just as Blair had predicted, it didn't take long for Cassie to find faces she not only recognized but was glad to see. She found that few of them had time to probe further into her life than "What do you do?" and "Where do you live?" unless more was volunteered. Some innocently asked "How many children do you have?" but when that was answered with an easy, "None," most put it down to independence and career. D.H. made another attempt at flirting, but Cassie was too distracted by what Sly was doing to notice or respond.

When the sun had found a niche almost directly overhead to beam down on the wilting people, Sly stood on a picnic table covered with empty potato chip bags and crusts of half-eaten sandwiches. Using the small PA system, he called for attention.

"Since I'm the class president, the reunion committee has given me the job of making all the announcements," he said over heckles and beer-loosened laughter. "It seems they've got some games prepared for the kids and the adults. The sign-up sheet is right here," he said, taking a piece of paper that was handed to him, "for... come on, this is a joke, right?" he asked, looking back at the vice president and the committee members. "A three-legged race. Couldn't you have been a little more creative?" He laughed, the pinkish tan darkening on his face beneath the harsh sun.

"What would you have preferred, Sly?" someone asked from the committee.

"Maybe a wet T-shirt contest?" Sly ventured, using his hand to stem the objections from the women and the whistles from the men.

His deep laughter against the microphone made the hairs on Cassie's neck rise. The sound brought back a barrage of memories that did nothing for her mood. A twinge of jealousy stung her.

"Let's see," he continued in a heavy baritone that sounded oddly intimate when amplified. "A pie-eating contest for the kids. And an arm wrestling contest for the men."

"What's the prize?" someone asked.

A diabolical smile lit Sly's scheming eyes. "A night alone with Lana Ricks."

A multitude of whistles and whoops sounded from the men being beaten playfully by their wives, and Cassie sought out the voluptuous body of the class's most available bachelorette. Lana was smiling beneath a swooping fringe of eyelashes that looked suspiciously false. She stood directly beneath Sly, offering him a private viewing of the full breasts that threatened to burst the seams of her tank top.

Cassie gritted her teeth, starting a headache that began to inch up from the base of her neck to her temples. Sly was laughing again, listing more of the games planned, following them with subtle jokes and innuendos that reminded her that he wasn't hers anymore. He was free, and though the things he said gave no indication that things were bad between them, they were cutting reminders to her.

When he'd come off his platform, he made his way to her in the crowd. "Having a good time?" he asked, his face startlingly attractive with the flush of heat coloring his tan.

Cassie smiled. "It's not as bad as I expected."

"Good. Because I signed us up for the three-legged race and the touch football game."

"You what?"

"I had to. Jerry bet me a million dollars I couldn't beat him. I couldn't turn down a challenge like that."

Cassie arched her brows. "You haven't got a million dollars."

"Neither has he." Sly chuckled. "But I still couldn't walk away from the challenge."

"Why me?" she moaned.

"Whom else would I have run with?" The question seemed genuine, but it gave Cassie little comfort.

"Lana Ricks, possibly."

A wry grin inched across Sly's face, and he glanced at the woman who was still waiting beside the table he had been standing on. "Believe me. It isn't as if she didn't try. But I think my chances are better with you. Her weight seems a little . . . out of proportion. It isn't distributed as well as yours."

If Cassie could have decided between slapping and strangling him, she would have responded. But she wasn't sure whether his comment about Lana's well-built top was a compliment or a put-down to her own more practically apportioned femininity. "I can't help it if I don't have overactive hormones."

Sly's seductive grin narrowed his eyes. "If I remember right, your hormones have always been just fine."

"About that three-legged race," Cassie said with an involuntary grin. "What do I have to do?"

"Just 'lean on me,'" Sly sang out. "Piece of cake."

Cassie couldn't help laughing at Sly's playful mood. "You're really having a good time, aren't you?"

"Sure, I am. Aren't you?"

"Of course," she answered, following him to where the other couples were preparing for the race.

The three-legged race was a hilarious attempt at competition, and the different sizes of couples tying their legs together made the game even funnier. Sly went at it with boyish enthusiasm, however, insisting that they lock bodies by holding each other around the waist, ordering Cassie to lean into him and completely surrender control of her inside leg.

"You're crazy," she told him when they were practicing. "I can't do that."

"Sure you can. Just imagine that it's asleep and let me control it."

His long-legged attempts at manipulating her shorter one proved ridiculous and nearly sent them tumbling into the grass a few times, and when Cassie sank into him laughing at their plight, he finally said, "All right, then. Use your own judgment."

The race became fun. It had been years since she and Sly had joined together in anything for one purpose. When the others dropped back to leave them neck and neck with Jerry and his wife, Sly ordered her to lean forward and barrel for the finish line. "Come on, baby," he shouted to her between breaths.

When they were first to touch the ribbon that was held by two children, he lifted her and whirled her around as if he'd just won the grand prix. Jerry admitted that he didn't really *have* the million dollars he had bet on the race, so Sly doubled the ante for the touch football game.

Because he was class president, Sly was captain of one team and Jerry led the other, both agreeing that the team with three touchdowns won. Cassie found herself playing on Sly's team, genuinely caught up by his competitive spirit. They were tied with two touchdowns each, when Sly cut a pass to Cassie, who caught the ball and tore across the grass. D.H. was blocking her, but Cassie ran faster with him at her heels, unable to reach her before she made the game point. Just as she crossed the touchdown line, however, D.H. threw his arms around her, pulling her down beneath him.

Before Cassie knew what had happened, Sly grabbed the back of D.H.'s collar, jerking it up with such force that three buttons popped off. "It's *touch* football, jackass!" Sly bit out. "We won the game, so you can quit trying to score!"

Cassie stood up, brushing off her legs. "Sly, it's all right. It's just a game."

D.H. raised his hands to calm Sly. "It was just done in fun," he said.

"Have fun with someone else's wife," Sly said, taking Cassie's hand and pulling her away from the crowd.

"That wasn't necessary," Cassie whispered, trying to sound annoyed, though a warm feeling coursed through her.

"Yeah, well..." He looked back to the crowd assembling around the tables. "I'm sorry. I guess I kind of got carried away."

"I think they're waiting for you," Cassie said, not knowing where to go from there. "Arm wrestling. You'll have to win this one without me."

"We do make a hell of a team," he answered with a provocative wink. "Forgiven?"

She smiled. "Forgiven. You'd better go get warmed up. The stakes are a little higher in this one, aren't they?"

Sly grinned at the reference to the "prize" of Lana Ricks, and started for the area where the men were lining up to prove their strength.

"I still can't get over how good he looks," Blair said, stepping up behind her as she stood watching him take his place at the table. "Some of us were talking about it. How does he do it? Jogging, weight lifting?"

Cassie turned back to Blair, not certain how to answer the question. She had wondered at it herself, for he had done none of those things when they'd been married. His virility was clearer to her now, though, and she was as curious as the others as to how he'd kept in shape. "A little of everything," she said finally.

"Do you work out with him?" Blair asked. "You've stayed in great shape, yourself."

"No," Cassie admitted. "I'm just on my feet a lot at work."

Blair gave a grateful laugh. "Great. It just comes naturally, right?"

Cassie shrugged. "What's your problem? You look like a model off the cover of *Vogue*."

Blair laughed. "Yeah, but it took me a year to get this way. Last summer when I realized I only had that amount of time to lose twenty pounds and firm up before our reunion, I joined a health club and actually *paid* them to abuse my body. This is the result."

"It seems to have been worth it, doesn't it?" Cassie teased.

"Not when someone like you walks up and says she didn't have to work at it. I mean, fair is fair." She laughed again, and glanced toward the arm wrestling table. "Is D.H. making a fool of himself?" she asked, her eyes on the two men in arm-to-arm combat.

Cassie didn't notice, for her eyes had drifted to Sly, who was now standing. His foot was propped on the bench, and he rested an elbow on his knee as he stood talking to Lana, whose body language was blatant.

"I see Lana's on the prowl," Blair said, shaking her head. "The girl always did have a thing for Sly."

Cassie tried to relax, and she slid her clenched hands into her pockets.

"If you're worried about it, why don't you go over there and intervene?" Blair suggested.

Cassie forced a laugh. "Worried?"

"Yes, 'worried.' You look like you could chew nails."

"Don't be ridiculous."

"All right, but if she were after my husband . . ."

Cassie made herself turn away. *But he's not my husband,* she wanted to shout to relieve the pressure. *He's nothing to me and I'm nothing to him, and I have no right to walk over there and scratch that little wimp's eyes out. . . .*

She felt her cheeks reddening and marched to the ice chest filled with water that had melted off the ice and fished out a beer. Popping the top, she took a gulp and turned back to the men. It was Sly's turn at the competition, and she watched as he took D.H.'s hand in his own, his eyes shooting psychological spears into his opponent. When the signal was given, she watched the controlled strength in his face and the strain of his bulging biceps and twisted forearms, his bare back rippling in the sunlight as he kept D.H.'s hand hovering at twelve o'clock. But before Sly had managed to dip the hands toward his side of the table, Cassie's eyes strayed to the woman leaning on the table beside Sly, her breasts clearly exposed from any angle, revealing through the thin fabric her own excitement at the struggle going on between the men. Her own panting cheers, Cassie was certain, provided just the incentive Sly needed to win.

A night alone with Lana Ricks, Cassie chanted to herself. Even though it had been said in jest, Lana would do what she could to carry out the promise, especially if Sly won.

The clasped fists hit the table with a thud, startling Cassie out of her bitter reverie, and she saw that Sly had won. She saw his eyes dart around the crowd until they found her, and a victorious thumb came up to stab the air. But before she had even returned the smile, Lana's arms were around his neck.

"I doubt Cassie will let you take your prize home, Sly," Lana said, with a sultry smile. "But maybe she won't mind a shortened version of what you would have won." With that, she planted a kiss on Sly's mouth, and the delighted crowd closed around them, blocking Cassie's view, for which she was painfully grateful.

Because she knew her classmates would expect some kind of response from her, and because she had never yet let a woman of Lana's caliber get the best of her, Cassie took a deep breath, raised her chin, and marched through the crowd. When she reached Sly, just coming up from Lana's assault, she tapped Lana on the shoulder and offered a saccharine smile. "Thanks for warming him up, Lana," Cassie said, at which the crowd hooted and whistled, "but Sly has spent all day compromising on his prizes. I'm not going to let all that hard work go unrewarded."

A delighted, anticipating grin twinkled in Sly's eyes, and he said nothing as Cassie sat in his lap, smiled warningly into his hooded eyes, and kissed him with all the fervor and passion she had been storing all day. His hand slid up her smooth leg and to her ribcage, his head moving pressure for pressure, his tongue doing a sexual dance against hers that only stirred but never sated. She could feel the pulse in his throat beating out an erotic message against her fingers. When she broke the kiss, the crowd applauded, but Sly's smile contradicted the desire in his eyes. "I'll collect the rest of that prize later," he told the crowd in a heavy voice, and everyone laughed freely.

Cassie left him as quickly as she had appeared when the attention was off her and Lana had left him for another potential conquest. Engaging in any conversation that would keep her from having to communicate with Sly, who couldn't seem to keep his eyes off her after her sudden display, Cassie learned everything there was to know about several different classmates, and still managed to seem interested in knowing more.

When the crowd began to thin out, Sly, still keeping an eye on her, sat down with the reunion committee to plan the awards for that evening. Cassie found Blair beside the swing set. Her daughter had climbed to the top and was shaking it in the hope that it would topple over. "If you hurt yourself I'll kill you!" she was shouting to the child. "If you think I'm afraid of taking you to the hospital and admitting that I broke every bone in your body with my bare hands, you're *wrong*."

Sighing with frustration when the child seemed not to hear, Blair turned back to the adults and smiled at Cassie. "Looks like you put Lana in her place," she said approvingly.

"It was a pleasure," Cassie admitted, still eyeing the child who had chosen to climb down via the chains that were holding the swings. "She's a bit active, isn't she?"

"And they wonder why I never had more," Blair moaned, grabbing her daughter by the waist and slinging her over her shoulder in mock anger. With a laugh, she nodded toward the committee. "I don't think Sly's mind is exactly on those awards," she said. "He can't keep his eyes off you."

"What?" Cassie asked, glancing at him. He smiled and lifted his hand in a wave.

"How do you do it? You two seem to lust after each other as much as you did back in high school. Isn't the volume supposed to tone down a little after all those years?"

A warm flush colored her cheeks. "Blair, come on. I don't know what you're talking about."

"I'm referring to those electric looks you've been giving each other all day. Like all you can think of is..."

"Don't be silly. You've been watching too many soap operas."

"That makes me an expert on the subject," Blair said, setting her free arm around Cassie's shoulder. "And I *know* passion when I see it."

Chapter Six

Cassie and Blair busied themselves cleaning off the picnic tables while they waited for the committee to break up. When they were finished, they fished two cold drinks out of the melting ice chest and sat down in the shade to watch the children who still played.

As Blair gossiped, Cassie glanced toward the committee and saw Sly's eyes on her again, his chin resting pensively on his hand while the others leaned together in deliberation. A chill went down her spine. Was it possible that he couldn't keep his mind off her, just as she was having trouble thinking of anything but him?

"Hello, you foxes," D.H. said, joining them in the shade. "Do I dare speak to you, Cassie? I don't think Sly has appreciated my attention to you today. If his actions didn't prove it, that little speech he gave me a while ago did."

A frown narrowed her eyes. "What did he say?"

"He told me, in no uncertain terms, that fifteen years didn't make you any less attached to him than before."

Cassie bit her lip and stared at D.H.'s shoes. It was true, she thought, but the callous way Sly pointed it out disheartened her. Vowing not to let it ruin her day, she pushed it out of her mind and arched her head back, letting a sudden breeze push the hair off her neck.

"Am I interrupting anything?" Sly asked from behind her. She looked up and saw his eyes engaging in combat with D.H. He had put on his shirt, and his black hair swung loose in its usual haphazard fashion.

"Just reminiscing," Blair said with a wry smile.

"Reminiscing," he repeated. He dropped his eyes to Cassie. "You ready to go yet?"

"Just waiting for you," she said.

Exchanging temporary good-byes until they would see each other again that evening, Cassie and Sly started across the lawn. "Did you have your blouse unbuttoned that much this morning?" he asked when he was helping her into the car.

Cassie glanced down at her blouse. "I guess so. Why?"

"Just wondered," he said, then closed the door.

When he got in, his face was taut and without expression. He started the car and pulled out of the parking lot.

"Why were you wondering about my blouse?" she prodded.

"Because you don't usually wear them open that much."

"How much?" she asked, vexation beginning to color her voice. "This is how I always wear it. Did I embarrass you or something?"

Sly's jaw popped, and she saw the whitening of his knuckles as he grasped the steering wheel. "What did that...what did he say to you?"

"What did who say?" The conversation was beginning to take on an unpredictable, irrational tone, and Cassie had no idea where it was leading.

"D.H."

Cassie thought a moment. "Not much. Why?"

"He's a lech and he's had the hots for you since you were sixteen."

Cassie laughed with disbelief. "Oh, come on. We were just talking."

"I don't want you talking to him."

The words were all Cassie needed to cross the threshold from uncertainty to anger. "Well, you don't have any say in the matter. I'll talk to anyone I please."

Sly's jaw popped. "We're supposed to look like a married couple. If you have to accept come-ons this weekend, you could at least have the decency to be discreet!"

Cassie's mouth fell open as his words penetrated. "How dare you!" she hissed, the scorching mist of anger stinging her eyes. She forced back her tears, refusing to break down in emotions in front of him. "You're the one who stood up in front of everyone and talked about wet T-shirt contests and nights alone with Lana Ricks! You call that discreet?"

"Everyone knew I didn't mean anything by it," he said, making a swinging turn that knocked Cassie against her door.

"*I* didn't know," Cassie shouted. "And I especially didn't know when you and Lana gave that little show for everyone. You want to talk about discreet?"

"I was trying to push her away," he said.

"Oh, sure you were. You had just won an arm wrestling contest with a two-hundred-pound man, but you couldn't seem to push one hundred twenty pounds of Lana Ricks away? Give me a break!"

"What was I supposed to do? Knock her down? *She* kissed *me*."

"If you're so concerned about covering cleavage, why didn't you ask little Lana to cover up a little more? You seemed to enjoy hers."

"She's not my wife!"

"You don't have a wife!" she screamed as he swung into another turn. "You're between wives, remember?"

Screaming silence filled the car like a lethal gas.

"Is that why you kissed me?" he asked finally in a softer voice.

"Is what why?" She really hadn't planned on discussing it, and she wanted more than anything just to forget the whole episode.

"To get back at Lana?"

Cassie rolled the answer around in her mind. Of course it had been to get back at Lana, but that need had come from the instinct to protect her territory. She didn't want anyone else's hands on Sly, and she didn't want Lana's kiss to be the last one that lingered on his lips when she saw him again. But she could never tell him that. "Why else would I have done it?"

She saw him swallow, and his face grew tighter. "I thought it might have had something to do with me," he said quietly.

The silence became too much for her, and she watched the houses on the road as they sped by. When she could stand it no more, her thoughts found voice. "Little witch would have been after you all these years if we'd stayed in Langston."

"What little witch?" he asked. "Lana?"

She frowned and didn't answer, keeping her eyes on the view outside the window. "Taking your shirt off didn't help any. It only added fuel to what was already a raging bonfire."

Sly's eyes came to life. "Come on. It was hot. Everybody had their shirts off."

"Everybody doesn't look like you," she said before she could catch herself.

The slightest grin softened Sly's lips as he pulled onto the gravel road that led to his house. "Everybody doesn't look like you, either," he said, "which is why I wanted your blouse buttoned a little higher."

"You didn't mention it when we left this morning," she said when he stopped the car in front of the house.

His smile curved his lips another degree. "I liked it this morning. It was just us." Their eyes met and held for a moment before he got out of the car and met Cassie on her side. He stopped her from going into the house by trapping her with an arm on each side of her shoulder, leaning into the car. "I like it now," he said, his breath a whisper on her lips. "And I liked it when you were in my lap and kissing me, whatever your motive was. But I didn't like everyone else imagining what was underneath."

Cassie wet her lips, and her eyes couldn't help dropping to his own. "I can't help what anyone imagines. Besides, why would anyone waste time imagining about me when Lana leaves so little to the imagination?"

Sly's grin cut across his face, releasing all his tension. "You *are* jealous of her, aren't you? You thought she was getting to me."

"Don't be ridiculous," Cassie said, infuriated that her thoughts showed so clearly on her face, hurt that he seemed to enjoy them so. "Why would I waste my time being jealous of Lana when I know for sure that you've been sleeping with Amanda and who knows whom else?"

When Sly caught his breath for a riposte, she broke out of his arms, starting toward the house. "This subject is getting boring," she choked, unable to take it further. "I'm going up to take a shower."

The pounding warmth of the water melted the ice around Cassie and drew all her emotions to the surface. How much more of him could she take? she wondered as she rinsed the last of the shampoo out of her hair and off her body. He could see through her, no matter what she said. And if he did, then he knew how much she wanted him.

Tears welled in her eyes and ran down her face to battle the drops of water from the shower. Once they started, they kept coming, tearing great chunks from her heart. Shaking with the weight of the tears, she

You know the thrill of escaping to a world of

EXOTIC LOCATIONS...
EXCITING ADVENTURE...
and ENDURING LOVE...

Escape again...with 4 FREE novels and

get more great Silhouette Romance novels —for a 15-day FREE examination— delivered to your door every month!

Travel the globe in search of romance—and find it in the pages of Silhouette Romance novels. You can escape month after month with such all-time favorite authors as Janet Dailey, Rita Rainville, Brittany Young, and Diana Palmer as your "guides."

Meet lively young heroines and share in their trials and triumphs...fascinating men you'll find as irresistible as the heroines do... and colorful supporting characters you'll feel you've known forever. They're all in Silhouette Romances—and now you can share every one of the wonderful reading adventures they provide.

FREE BOOKS

Start today by taking advantage of our special offer—4 brand new Silhouette Romance novels (a $7.80 value) *absolutely FREE* along with a free Mystery Gift. Just fill out and mail the attached order card.

AT-HOME PREVIEWS, FREE DELIVERY

After you receive your 4 free books and Mystery Gift, every month you'll have the chance to preview 6 more Silhouette Romance novels *as soon as they are published.* When you decide to keep them, you'll pay just $11.70, *with never an additional charge of any kind and with no risk!*

Cancel your subscription at any time simply by dropping us a note. In any case, the first 4 books and Mystery Gift are yours to keep.

EXTRA BONUS

When you take advantage of this offer, we'll also send you the Silhouette Books Newsletter FREE with each shipment. Every informative issue features news about upcoming titles, interviews with your favorite authors, and even their favorite recipes.

Get a Free
Mystery Gift, too!

EVERY BOOK YOU RECEIVE WILL BE A BRAND-NEW FULL-LENGTH NOVEL!

Escape with 4 Silhouette Romance novels (a $7.80 Value) and get a Mystery Gift, too!

Silhouette Romance®

Silhouette Books, 120 Brighton Rd., P.O. Box 5084, Clifton, NJ 07015-9956

Yes, please send me 4 FREE and without obligation, 4 brand new Silhouette Romance novels along with my Mystery Gift. Unless you hear from me after I receive my 4 FREE books, please send me 6 new Silhouette Romance novels for a free 15-day examination each month as soon as they are published. I understand that you will bill me a total of just $11.70, with no additional charges of any kind. There is no minimum number of books that I must buy, and I can cancel at any time. The first 4 books and Mystery Gift are mine to keep, even if I never take a single additional book.

NAME _____
                  (please print)

ADDRESS _____

CITY _____ STATE _____ ZIP _____

hugged her arms across her chest and dropped to the floor of the bathtub, letting the water beat down on her lowered head as she sobbed with greater force than she had in all her life.

Where had they lost it, she wondered with great regret? They had been so happy, so in love, but one morning she had awakened filled with numbness and emptiness. The numbness had seemed comforting after the baby's death, so she had clung to it, letting it dictate her life for months afterward. But the numbness had cost her Sly. And even that loss had seemed fitting in the context of her life at the time.

But what about now? She wanted him now, desired him with more fervor than she ever had. He could be hers this weekend, for he had made it clear that he still desired her, too. But what would happen after the weekend? Cassie didn't have the luxury of numbness anymore. She would feel the twisting stab in her heart when Sly went back to Chicago—back to marry Amanda. Making love to him now would only take her back, make her relive the pain in living color as she lost him again when the time came.

But was she strong enough to turn him away the next time he brought his lips hauntingly close to hers? And how would she sleep beside him tonight and not touch him?

Taking a final deep, sobbing breath, Cassie dipped her face in the water that was now turning cool and let it rinse away the evidence of her love for Sly. She turned off the water and pulled herself up to get out, patting her hair with the towel, then wrapping it around her.

She was alone in the house, except for Sasha, who was napping in her room downstairs. Everyone else had gone their separate ways, and when she had run into the house, she had seen Sly heading for the pond to take a walk. Silence gripped her. The same silence she would go home to tomorrow. The same silence she had come to dread like age or death or any of the other destinies that life had to offer.

Opening the door, she felt the cool air from the air conditioner sweep the steam off her shoulders. Going to the dresser just outside the door, she picked up her brush and ran it through the long wet strands, slicking it back from her face as she gazed blindly into the mirror. Why couldn't she just abandon yesterday and tomorrow and cling to today as if it were her last moment on earth? she asked herself. Why couldn't she allow herself the luxury of Sly's attentions one more time?

Setting the brush down, she raked her fingernails through the thick wet mass of hair and arched her back to relax the tension and fatigue while she turned toward the bed. Her heart and mind and hands froze when she saw Sly lying there, hands behind his head, gazing at her as if she were nothing more than a beautiful vision blown in by the steam.

Her hands came down and she clutched the top of her towel. "What are you doing here?"

"I didn't mean to scare you," he said without his usual trace of amusement. "I thought I'd lie down a while. I—"

"You could have said something," she said, trying to control her breathing.

"I was as surprised as you," he said in a soft, soothing voice. "I didn't expect—"

"Didn't you?"

"No, I really thought—"

"I know what you thought."

"You don't know what I thought." Pulling himself up to sit on the edge of the bed, he gazed at her, and his eyes dropped to the damp sheen of her shoulders and the column of her neck and made their slow, sweeping journey across the curve of her breasts covered by the towel. A paralyzing moment passed as their eyes locked, silently revealing every naked thought that passed between them.

Slowly, Sly stood up, until he was looking down into her face. The race in her heart drained the strength from Cassie's legs, and she was powerless to move. "I'll get dressed in the bathroom," she whispered from deep in her throat.

"Don't," he said, taking her wrist with his hand. She stopped, as if his order finalized things. His thumb moved over the small blue cords of her wrist, and his eyes told her he could feel his effect on her in her pulse. "How much longer are you going to keep this up?" he asked, the breath of his words on her face sending a shiver down her spine.

"Keep what up?"

He stared at her for an explosive moment, the hold of his eyes stopping the world for as long as she gazed back. She could see the strain on his face, feel it in the heat radiating from him. Wetting his lips, he took her by the shoulders, his hands trembling against her bare skin. On a swallow, he said, "God, Cass. Don't you know you're driving me crazy?"

Cassie found that her body gave her no choice but to stand face to face with him. He seemed to inch closer, until there was no distance at all between them. "I'm not trying to," she whispered.

"You don't have to try," he replied. "All you have to do is stand there, and I feel—"

Her head rolled back as he spoke, the offering of her lips cutting off his words. His lips hovered over hers for a moment, his eyes searching the farthest corners of her heart to find the answers. Slowly, his lips closed over hers, gently, at first, nipping the corners of her mouth and moving across the full pout of her lips until his mouth opened and closed on hers, coaxing her to join in the madness. When their tongues came together, it was with a savoring slowness that drew need from Cassie's heart that she'd never known she had. She felt her hands scaling the muscles of his chest, sliding around his shoulders and alighting in the hair that curled over his collar. His hands pressed her closer against him, and one fell to the soft curve of her hip. Her hips lifted forward and found the center of his desire, pressing against it until her own core throbbed for his touch. His fingers reached the bottom of her towel and feathered up her smooth thigh, sparking trembling energy in her that told her she had no choice but to love him.

With quivering breaths, he left her mouth and slid his lips down her throat and across her shoulders, his arms wrapping around her hips to pull her as tight as she could be against him. She closed her eyes and rolled her head backward, telling him with her body that there would be no turning back.

But he stopped and took her by the shoulders again, pulling her away from him and gazing into her eyes with smoky-blue ones hooded by his thick sweeping lashes. His breathing came deep and rapid. "You don't know what you're doing to me, Cass," he whispered breathlessly. "Be sure before—"

She touched his lips with her fingertip to silence him, and he took it in a trembling hand and pressed it against his face, gazing at her with fierce yearning. He pulled the shirt out of his shorts, and lifted her other hand. With his eyes studying hers for a hint of hesitance, he set her hand on his stomach and slid it slowly upward with his own, through the soft, curling mass of hair, across the nipple sharp with arousal, and stopped over his heart where she could feel the extent of his need. With great effort it seemed, he swallowed, and she lowered her hand to his waist.

As if he could stand no more, his eyes dropped to the towel tucked between her breasts. Her own heart threatened to escape as his hands came up and his fingers lifted the corner out. Slowly, he unwrapped her and let the towel drop. A deep moan came like a breath from his throat as his hands outlined her body without touching it, trembling to feel the flesh, but refusing to make contact, as if it would disappear if he did.

His lips were the first to touch her again, and this time the kiss was deep and demanding, though he kept his body apart from hers. She knew he feared what had happened the night before—that she would take him to the brink and stop him—so she claimed control and became the aggressor. Sliding his shirt up his chest, she stepped toward him until the peaked nipples of her breasts crushed against his chest. She could feel the restrained passion quivering inside him, and keeping her green eyes on his, she pulled the shirt over each arm and slid it over his head.

His hands closed around her head, sliding down the wet hair that adorned her as if she'd planned it specifically for this. Eyes still locked with his, she ventured toward his zipper, unclasped the snap, and slowly pulled it down. Slipping her hands in the back of his pants, she slid them down over his hips, holding her breath. He pulled her against him then, kissing her with a ravaging force that made her legs feel boneless as he sank to the bed, pulling her above him.

Her breasts tickled as they brushed against him, but the feel of his need against her lower body distracted her. As if he were refusing to join in the agony of her game, he took her fiercely by the shoulders and rolled her onto her back, his mouth devastating her as he bit his way down her neck and trailed to a nipple, licking hot flames across it that made her close her eyes and groan as he played her with the strength and control that had haunted her dreams.

Suddenly, when she thought she could wait no longer, he filled her. More than two years of passion overflowed in a very short time as he carried her to the galaxy where ecstasy reigns. Tiny explosions led to larger ones, until the greatest of all dampened every pore in her body and made her moan his name in a distant voice that floated into eternity. He kept the magic alive, even after they were sated, moving against her until his own fatigue could no longer be gainsaid.

The weight of his body still on hers, he pushed the wet strands of hair out of her face and gazed into her eyes. Sudden reality overwhelmed Cassie, and her contented smile faded slowly as she saw the tenderness on his face. Without warning, tears welled in her eyes, and a large, traitorous one dipped over her lashes and rolled down her cheek.

Chapter Seven

Concern deepened Sly's blue eyes as his thumb stroked the damp path of the tear that was disappearing into her hair. "Regrets?" he asked on a soft breath.

Cassie shook her head, unable to speak for fear it would open the floodgates through which that one tiny drop had escaped.

"What then?" he whispered. His body was still anchoring Cassie's, and she felt life pulsing inside him, warm life, vibrant life that heated Cassie's blood and that she did not want to let go. "My Cassie never cries. It must be serious."

"I'm not crying," she muttered as another tear escaped and ran down her other cheek.

New lines creased between Sly's brows and around the outer corners of his eyes. "Tell me," he entreated. "I need to understand you."

How could he understand, when she didn't understand herself?

"Just hold me," she whispered. "Don't let me go just yet."

"I never want to let you go," he whispered, pushing her hair back, the slow rhythm of his breathing pressing his stomach into hers. "I could lie like this forever, just holding you and looking at you. You're so beautiful, Cass. So special." His own eyes misted at his words, and Cassie's threatened to overflow until she closed them to stop the tears.

His body moved above hers, shifting until his mouth was on her eyelids, kissing away the tears that were creeping between her lashes and trickling down her face. "Look at me," he ordered quietly.

She opened her eyes, her spiked lashes providing a lacy frame for the green pool of tears. His own eyes were narrowed, drawing her out of herself and into him so he could probe and study her at length.

"These aren't tears of joy. You're sad, and I have to know why. In all the years I've known you, I've never known you to cry. Come on, Cass. Tell me what's wrong."

Pulling out from under him, Cass sat up on the bed and picked up the towel, draping it around her nakedness again. "We're not married anymore, Sly. We shouldn't have let it go that far."

Sly slid up and put a warm hand on each of her shoulders. "Did I take advantage? Did I make you do it against your will?" he asked quietly.

Slowly, she shook her head. Turning on the bed to face him, she touched his chest and let her fingers run through the soft, curling mass of dark hair. "I wanted you," she said simply.

"Then what's the problem?" he asked. "We both wanted it. We may be divorced, but I've never been able to think of you as anything but my wife. And I can't believe that you don't still think of me as your husband."

Cassie took a deep breath and stood up, went to the dresser, and ran a brush through her hair, which was beginning to dry in feathery wisps around her face. She set the brush down, then turned back to Sly who was waiting on the bed, one foot on the floor, the other hidden behind the rumpled bedspread. "I'd be a fool to think of you as my husband," she said stiffly. "I'm not up to that kind of pain."

"What kind of pain?" he asked. "Have I hurt you?"

"No," she said quickly. "It's just that I don't think either of us should blow what just happened out of proportion. You have sexual needs that aren't accustomed to going unsated. We filled needs for each other, and..."

"What the hell are you talking about?" he asked, rising and snatching his shorts off the floor. Yanking them on, he glared at Cassie.

"I just mean that I don't plan to be your playmate after being your wife."

"My playmate?" The word sounded absurd when he repeated it.

"Yes. It's no secret that you're engaged, or that your love life has been vigorous between commitments—"

"You must be kidding."

"I'm not kidding, Sly. I know all about you. It's okay, because it has no effect on me one way or another. I just want to make it clear that I have no intention of being another notch in your belt."

"Another notch! Lady, you were the *only* notch for the first thirty-two years of my life. And frankly, I'm surprised that you had time to keep up with mine in light of your own."

Cassie felt a foreboding tightness gripping her at his accusatory tone, and she lifted her chin defensively. "What do you mean?"

"I mean that I haven't exactly been kept in the dark about your love life either. I know all about that male model you went to Paris with, and I know about the lawyer and the C.P.A. and the journalist— Would you like for me to go on, or have I made my point?"

Cassie was stunned. She had gone out with all of those men in the past year, but none of those dates had gone farther than the front door of her apartment. Even her kisses had been mere pecks on the cheek, for she hadn't wanted to get involved with any of them. The trip to Paris had been strictly business, and despite the man's efforts, she had not allowed any of his advances to go anywhere. "How did you know about those?"

"The same way you knew, I suspect. Frank loves to gossip. It makes me wonder if he has ulterior motives."

"It wasn't exactly gossip," Cassie said in self-defense. "There was nothing to tell about any of those men."

"Nothing to tell? I doubt that, Cass," he said, his words tumbling out in anger. "But what does it matter whom you sleep with? We don't owe each other explanations anymore. We're nothing to each other. We simply wound up together here, and we both happened to need a good roll in the hay at the same time. Isn't that right?''

The articulation of all her fears, even when flung in sarcasm, stung Cassie. She had known the aftermath would be painful, but she had never expected it to be so bitter. The bitterness formed a sick knot in her stomach, and her face grew hot and strained. How dared he believe she had been frivolous with her body simply because he had done it himself?

With fury rising to burn out reason, Cassie stepped toward Sly, a trembling hand clenching into a fist. ''How dare you assume that I've been as promiscuous as you?''

Sly stood firmly facing her, his lips an angry slash across his face, his feet slightly apart. ''I'm just going by the information I was given.''

''Then your information was wrong! I've slept with one man in my life, Sly! One man! Figure that one out.''

Sly brought his hands to his hips and glanced away as if turning her words over in his mind. Deep lines etched between his brows and ran from his nose to the corners of his mouth. In a less convinced voice, he said, ''Then maybe your information was wrong, too.''

The words were almost a denial, and sent Cassie into a rage that she had no will to control. ''I might have questioned it—'' her words grated through clenched teeth ''—if I hadn't stumbled on it first-hand.'' The statement flew across the room like fuel spilling on every surface it reached, its fatal fumes rising into the air, awaiting the spark that would set it aflame.

Sly's face contorted further as he struggled to grasp her meaning. "Firsthand? How? Do you mean that newspaper article last week?"

"No. I mean *firsthand*," she retorted, her words springing to life like the bonfire that resulted from a careless match. "I came back to you, Sly. A few months ago, after the divorce, I came back to you! You never knew it because you were busy upstairs—in our bedroom!"

Sly's anger fell from him like something tangible, and his eyes grew round and dull. "You came back? Why didn't you—?"

"It seemed a little awkward to walk in and say hello, under the circumstances." She bit the words out. "I decided, instead, to go back to New York and put our life completely behind me."

A crackling, sizzling moment passed between them as two pairs of eyes filled with pain locked together, despite the compulsion to look away. After a while, Sly ran a trembling hand through his dark hair and slid it down his face, rough with stubble. "Who... whom was I with?" he asked in a shaken, broken voice.

The question was like ice water flung on the heart of the flame, encompassing Cassie in strangling smoke. "Who the hell knows, Sly? Who the hell cares if there were so many that you can't even remember? Amanda must be a fool to get tied up with you!" Fresh tears filled her eyes and throat, burning, stinging tears that she slapped away in defiance. Jerking out a drawer, she grabbed her clothes and stormed toward the bathroom to dress in private. "And I guess that just makes me an idiot, too. At least before I was your wife. Now I'm just one more in a long string of lovers!"

"Cassie!" he shouted as the door slammed in his face.

Cassie dressed in thirty seconds, biting back the sobs of anger at herself for telling him of her vulnerability and at him for making it so real. When she opened the door, her tears had stopped. He was leaning against the frame, elbow above his head, covering his brow with his hand. "Cass, we were divorced. I never knew you wanted—"

"It doesn't matter," she said, going to the closet and pulling out the dress she had brought to wear that evening. "We were divorced. We still are. You get married again, go on with your life. None of it matters, anymore."

"Where are you going?" he asked when she opened the door. "We need to talk about this."

"Talk?" she asked on a dry, humorless laugh. "Why? What difference will it make?" She looked down at the dress draped over her arm, the shoes hanging from her fingers. "I need to spend some time with my family while I'm here," she said, avoiding meeting the pleading, sorrowful eyes that held her. "I'll walk over and you can pick me up there tonight."

"Are you sure you want to go on with this?" he asked, and the dull note of his voice told her he was offering her a way out. It was up to her. They could abandon the whole charade, tell the truth, fly back to their separate homes.... The thought seemed even more dismal than the scene they'd just experienced, and for the first time she realized that it was not for Sasha that she had kept the divorce a secret. It was for herself, for in clinging to the lie she had, in a sense, been able to hold on to Sly and to the best part of herself.

Bringing her eyes back to his, she nodded. "Why destroy everyone's image of the perfect marriage? Tomorrow it'll all be over, and I'll leave it up to you and Amanda to break the news." Then she left him there, closing the door to shut off her view of the man who was as steeped with regrets as she was herself. Why couldn't she hate him? she wondered, leaning back against the closed door. After a year, why couldn't she at least stop loving him?

Heaving a deep breath, Cassie wiped the dampness off her face and started down the stairs, praying under her breath that no one had come home during their fight and that no one would stop her as she left.

But no sooner had she started across the hollow wooden floor of the living room than a deep, raspy voice summoned her from Sasha's room. "That you, Cassandra?"

Cassie stepped to the open doorway of the bedroom and peered in to see the old woman reclining on her bed. "I thought you were sleeping," she said in a soft voice.

"Come here and sit down," Sasha ordered, emphasizing her request with her shaking hands. "I heard angry voices upstairs," she said bluntly as Cassie obeyed. "Either I was having a nightmare, or you and Sly were fighting."

Cassie tried to smile. "We weren't fighting, Sasha."

"I may be old," Sasha argued on a huff of breath, "but I'm not deaf nor stupid. I didn't hear the particulars of the fight, but I can guess."

Cassie sank back defeatedly and smoothed out the dress still hanging on her arm. "All right, Sasha. We had a little disagreement. It's over now, though. Nothing serious."

The old woman turned on her side and pushed herself up until she sat face to face with Cassie. "Nothing serious," she mimicked in an unflattering voice. "I see what's going on with you and Sly. Young lady, marriage can be a very fragile thing. If you put too many cracks in it, it'll shatter right in your fingers. You and Sly are having problems, aren't you?"

Cassie was shocked at the perception of the tiny woman before her, but now that the opportunity was presenting itself, she couldn't manage to admit to her failed marriage. Her lie was the one thread connecting her to Sly. She wasn't yet ready to let it go before its time. "Why do you say that?" she asked.

"You can't talk to each other," Sasha said gruffly. "You're not comfortable with each other."

"We are," Cassie started to argue, but Sasha nipped her words.

"It's the baby, isn't it?" she asked, the lines deepening by degrees on her face as she leaned closer to Cassie. She set her hands on Cassie's knees.

Cassie swallowed and focused her eyes on the old woman's gnarled, thin hands. "No," she whispered.

"Yes," Sasha said. "Don't deny it to yourself, girl! The death of your baby took something from you that couldn't be replaced."

Cassie cleared her throat and moved to leave. "I can't talk about this with you."

"Then don't talk," Sasha said sternly, her grip on Cassie's knees tightening. "Just listen. I know how you feel, Cassie. I'm not so old that I can't remember how it feels to lose a child."

Cassie's troubled, moist eyes shot up to meet Sasha's misty gray ones. "You . . . you lost a child?"

The tremor in Sasha's face and hands seemed accelerated, but her voice was steady as she spoke. "I lost my first born to the flu epidemic in 1918," Sasha said, holding Cassie's eyes. "It never stops hurting. The unfairness *never* goes away. But you have your husband, Cassie. I see a rift between you, but I also see that you still love each other very much—maybe more than before because you've shared a loss that no one else will ever understand."

Cassie couldn't answer. Grief choked her, and she covered her face with a hand. Memories and needs enclosed her in darkness, leaving her blind and alone. "If you've been through it, then you know. I love you, Sasha, but I can't—"

"Can't talk about it," Sasha said more gently. "If you guard it like a treasure you think you'll somehow be making up for it. Whatever you did wrong, whatever you didn't do, whatever Sly may have done—"

"I don't blame Sly for Laura's death," she blurted, realizing it was the first time she had used the baby's name.

"Then tell him," Sasha urged. "It's surfacing, Cassie. You can hide it just so long before it takes hold of you when you least expect it. Grieve, cry, share it with your husband before it ruins you. And then go on with your life, for God's sake. Your husband needs you, child. It was his baby, too. He has his own demons.''

Cassie's hand slid to cover her twisted mouth, and she gazed at the beloved old woman through a blur of tears. "It wasn't the same for hìm," she said. "It wasn't like he realized the baby was real. For so many years while we were trying to conceive, the baby was just an idea, a dream. And when she died, it was no more than the death of an idea to him. Not the death of a child.''

"How can you say that?" Sasha asked, slamming a frail hand onto her mattress. "I don't know what led you to those insane ideas of yours, but I know my grandson. He doesn't let go easily of things he loves. You can't assume how he felt, anymore than he can assume how you felt." She lowered her head to the pillow again and pulled her legs back up. "You young people are so exhausting," she hissed.

Cassie wiped her eyes and studied the resting body of the old woman. "Are you okay, Sasha?" she asked hesitantly.

"I'm not dying, if that's what you mean, Cassie. Just tired. You can count on me being around at least as long as it takes to see things right with you and Sly again. Life is too precious to waste on selfish sorrows. It isn't your sorrow alone." Letting out a heavy sigh, Sasha closed her eyes.

"I'll go now and let you sleep," Cassie said quietly, feeling relieved and deprived at the same time, as if her hour in the psychiatrist's office were up. When Sasha didn't answer, she left the room, closing the door behind her.

Chapter Eight

The mile-long walk to her parents' house gave Cassie ample time to recapture the fragile numbness that had helped her survive the worst periods of her life. After several hours with her family, and several glasses of her father's homemade wine, her spirits even began to lighten. She sat on the front porch with her parents, her oldest brother, Jack, and her younger sister, Barbara. Three of her nieces, who lived nearby, played in an inflated swimming pool in the front yard, splashing and dunking each other, while the two nephews engaged in a garden hose battle.

"I hear Sly got a little hot under the collar at the picnic today," Jack said, grinning teasingly at Cassie.

"About what?" she asked. The picnic seemed weeks ago, and so much had happened since then that she barely remembered it.

"When D.H. tackled you. I ran into him in town after it was all over, and he told me what happened."

"Nothing happened," Cassie said.

"Didn't sound like 'nothing' to me. D.H. said Sly literally tore the shirt off his back pulling him off of you."

"D.H. always did love a drama. If I remember, his shirt was perfectly intact, except for maybe a button or two that popped off."

Jack leaned his head back and let out a boisterous laugh. The others joined him, but Cassie failed to see the humor. "Old Sly always did have a sore spot when it came to D.H. and you."

Exasperation colored Cassie's cheeks. "There was never a 'D.H. and me.'"

"Didn't you go out with him once?" Barbara asked.

Cassie nodded. "When Sly and I broke up once for a few weeks, I did. But it never meant much."

"Sly never forgot it," Jack said on a laugh. "Kept him on his toes for years."

Cassie's mother let out a long sigh. "Yes, but Cassie and Sly always had eyes for each other. No one else could get close. I used to worry, when they were so young, that they didn't go out with other people."

"Hell," her father chimed in. "When you two announced that you were getting married when you were just kids—"

"They were twenty-one," Barbara cut in in defense of her sister.

"I'll admit I was a little shaken up. I knew you were head over heels for each other, but I didn't know it would last. Once again, I was wrong."

Cassie let her eyes drift out over the yard to the children playing. Even here, in the solace of her childhood home, she could not escape Sly. If she told them they had divorced, would they leave his name out of their conversations? And would that be any more comfort, considering that she had no past at all if she cut out the parts that included Sly?

Excusing herself, Cassie went into the cool house and walked from room to room, looking for traces of the home she once had known. It didn't seem like home anymore. It was smaller and older. The house she had shared with Sly had been home for her. That had been her life.

Walking into the bedroom she had long ago given up to Barbara, Cassie sat on the bed and stared at a chip in the paint on the wall. Sly had asked her if she had regrets. Now, looking around the room that seemed strange to her after so many years, she knew she did. But they had nothing to do with making love with Sly today. She did not regret that, for it was something of him to remember. Something that warmed her blood, even though it made her heart ache. Her regrets were based on the way she had let her marriage die with the baby. The way she had held in her pain, while she had desperately needed to lash out at Sly for accepting the stillbirth with such strength. How had he survived that loss unscathed? How had he been able to act as if nothing had changed?

The telephone rang, startling Cassie out of her reverie. Someone downstairs answered it, then called up, "Cassie! It's Sly!"

Cassie looked at the phone on Barbara's bed table, reaching carefully for it as if it were a live, threatening being. Her hand trembled as she brought it to her ear, and Sly's soft voice on the other end made her heart miss a beat. "Cass? Are you okay?" he asked.

"Fine." She cleared her throat.

"I . . . I talked to Sasha just now," he said.

"Did you tell her?"

"No. Not the truth. She knows things aren't right between us, though."

"I know. She told me."

A moment of thoughtful silence followed, and finally Sly spoke again. "She got me started thinking about. . .things. I've made mistakes, Cass. Maybe I've ruined things for good."

"It takes two people to ruin a marriage," Cassie said quietly.

"I never wanted to let you go," Sly said, his voice cracking with the admission. "If I had known for a minute that you wanted to come back, I never would have . . . everything would have been different."

"Maybe it's best that everything turned out the way it did," Cassie said without conviction.

"I don't believe that," he whispered. "I hope you don't believe it, either."

Cassie couldn't answer. Already a tear was running down her face and across the fingers that were clutching the receiver. She had cried more today than she had in her entire life, she thought. Would she be able to stop all the feeling tomorrow when she went back home?

"I'll pick you up at seven," he said in a dejected voice.

"Okay," Cassie said, nodding her head as if he could see her. "I'll see you then."

"Cass?" His voice came in a whisper, just before she started to put the phone in its cradle.

"Yes?"

"I'm still in love with you."

The statement hung like a nuclear bomb frozen in midair, bringing terrifying reality to light. Her throat constricted. Her heart stopped. Moments passed before she could respond to the startling statement, and before she had time to speak, a click told her Sly was gone.

Staring at the phone, she listened as the dial tone hummed out its finality. Was she surprised that he still loved her? she asked herself. Hadn't she known deep down that he still cared? But love had never really been the problem, she reminded herself.

Maybe Sasha was right. Maybe Sly did need her. Maybe she had buried herself with the baby, so deeply that only now could she let herself come back and feel those emotions she'd held at bay for so long. She had come out of that cave for a short while today when she had loved Sly. The light of his passion had been brilliant, if blinding, and now the shadows that had become her reality would never be sufficient again. Loneliness would never be a comfort. But Amanda still remained, and so did the hostility she could not help feeling over his flippant attitude after the baby's birth.

"What's wrong?" Barbara asked from the doorway of her room. "You've been down in the dumps since you got off that plane. Are you and Sly having problems?"

The fact that she was so transparent irked her. "Why is it that every time someone thinks I'm down they automatically assume it has to do with Sly? Look at me. I'm one person. Can't I have feelings that don't tie me to him?''

The startled look on Barbara's face made Cassie instantly regret her words. "Sorry," her sister said. "I just thought you might want to talk.''

"I've talked enough today," Cassie said, pushing past her to leave the room. She stopped before she was completely through the door, and turned back to her sister, who stood frozen as if she had been slapped for no reason. "I'm sorry," Cassie said, covering her face with trembling hands. "I didn't mean to jump on you. It's just that sometimes..." Her voice trailed off as fresh tears sprang into her eyes. "I've turned into a regular tear-factory this weekend. I don't know what's wrong with me.''

Concern knitted Barbara's brows. "I've always been your kid sister, Cassie, but I'm a grown woman now. If you need to talk, I'm here.''

Cassie looked at the ceiling, wondering how much longer she could go on without talking to someone. Barbara, who had always been the tomboy who tattled on everyone, was indeed a grown woman. She could trust her now, and she desperately needed to trust someone. Over a heavy sob, she said, "Don't ever fall in love, Barbara.''

"It's too late." Barbara smiled, sitting on the edge of the bed. "You know I already have." A moment of silence rang between them, and finally Barbara chanced a question, her smile fading. "Have you found someone else?''

A slow frown wrinkled Cassie's brows. "Someone else? No.''

"Then it's still Sly you're in love with."

A lump formed in Cassie's throat, and nodding silently, she closed the bedroom door and leaned against it, facing her sister.

"Has he found someone else?"

Cassie pressed the heel of her hand to her eyes. "It's not that simple."

Barbara stood up and heaved a deep breath. "Cassie, he's your husband. Has he been unfaithful or hasn't he?"

Cassie shook her head. "First, he is not my husband."

"Of course, he is."

"No." A sob punctuated the word. "We divorced a year ago. After... after the baby."

Barbara sucked in a disbelieving breath and Cassie watched the color drain from her face. "No. You can't have. You... I..."

"We couldn't tell anyone," Cassie said, dropping her hands, "because we were worried about Sasha. And I couldn't bear to go through it with the family."

"So this weekend... all of it is a lie?"

Cassie felt the way she had felt years ago when she'd been the one to let slip to Barbara that there was no such thing as Santa Claus. What was she telling her now, just weeks before her wedding? That there was no such thing as sustaining love? Dismally, she nodded her head in answer to her sister's whispered question.

"I can't believe it." Barbara sank to the edge of the bed and seemed to struggle with her own emotion, and she blinked back the silver wave of tears in her eyes. "Cassie, what happened? You were happy. I could see it. Tell me the truth, Cassie. You *were* happy once, weren't you? I didn't imagine it, did I?"

The question seemed so important to Barbara, that Cassie had no choice but to be honest. "We were happy, Barbara. And I'm not sure what happened." She took a deep breath that seemed to fill her with the energy to go on. "After the baby we stopped talking. Sly began to spend all of his time at work, and when he came home I just wanted to be left alone. One or both of us just quit caring. And the next thing I knew I was flying off to Mexico for a divorce."

"Mexico?" Barbara whispered as if she couldn't bear to say it aloud.

Cassie closed her eyes. "I wanted to save us both the agony of an Illinois divorce. I was desperate to put all the pain behind me as fast as I could. When I came back, I moved to New York."

Barbara's eyes left Cassie and focused on the wall as she assimilated the harsh facts. After a while, her eyes brightened, and she sat up straight. "But you said you still love him. If you do, isn't there a chance that you two could—"

"No, Barbara," Cassie said. "A lot has happened since then. A lot has changed. Last week he and his new lover became engaged."

"But you still love him!"

Cassie bowed her head wearily and focused on her sandals. "Sometimes love isn't enough."

Her sister's dry laugh followed, and Barbara stood up and walked around the bed to peer out the window. "Then what does that leave me?"

Cassie went to her and put an arm around her shoulder. "It won't be the same. You won't let it happen to you."

Barbara turned back to Cassie, new hope in her eyes. "You're going to get back together, Cassie. He isn't married, yet. Maybe this weekend is just the thing to do it. Maybe—"

Cassie was shaking her head. "I can't count on that, Barbara. I'm not even sure if I want it."

Barbara's tears spilled over her lashes and she banged a fist into the wall. "It *has* to happen, Cassie. If I can't believe in you and Sly, then what on earth *can* I believe in?"

"Believe in yourself," Cassie said, taking her sister by the shoulders. "You have to take responsibility for your own love. You can't see Sly and me or anyone else as role models. We'll fall short every time."

"I'm not talking about role models, Cassie. I'm talking about the sacred institution of marriage, with vows exchanged before God, with two people who love each other knowing how serious that commitment is. I'm talking about the love you and Sly have had for each other since I was a little girl. It wasn't all a dream, Cassie. You can get it back if you try."

Cassie let the words penetrate, and her eyes drifted back to the telephone. "He told me he still loves me, just now on the phone," she murmured.

"Then don't let him go again. If you let this chance go then you deserve it if someone else comes along for him. I'll help you."

"How can you help?" Cassie asked with exasperation.

"I can make sure that when he picks you up to-night you knock his socks off. And I can make sure that you don't sit around here and mope the rest of the day. Come on. We don't have much time."

"But Barbara, I'm not even sure if I want to knock his socks off."

"You don't have a choice," Barbara said, pulling trays of makeup out of her top dresser drawer. "Just shut up and do what I say. You can't be objective. I can."

And before Cassie could object again, Barbara had pushed her into a chair and was slapping cold cream on her face.

Cassie found that she was too nervous to eat a bite when the family gathered at the table. Her makeup had been applied to Barbara's satisfaction, and her head was covered with rollers that Barbara had insisted on putting in herself to "give it enough body," even though Cassie intended to wear it up.

"Be careful not to smudge your fingernail polish when you eat that," Barbara warned when Cassie picked up a bread stick at the table.

"Leave her alone, for heaven's sake," their mother said. "I dare say Cassie knows how to eat with finger-nail polish on."

"But it's not dry!"

"Leave her alone," her mother repeated. "You'd think she was getting ready for the senior prom, the way you're fussing over her."

Cassie laughed. "I think she's paying me back for all the times I worried over her when she was getting ready for things. I deserve it, I suppose."

"Well, she's giving me a headache and making me nervous." Playfully, her mother looked at her youngest daughter and wagged a finger at her. "You just wait until that wedding of yours. When you start yelling for me to leave your hair alone and not touch your makeup, I'm going to remind you of this."

Everyone laughed, and Cassie was glad she had confided in her sister. It had taken a tremendous burden off her shoulders, and the flurry of preparations Barbara had started had drawn her into the magic and terror of looking Sly in the eye for the first time since he'd told her he loved her. The thought sent little butterflies fluttering around in her stomach, and Cassie couldn't remember the last time she'd been so nervous. "I'm sorry," she said, finally. "But I'm really not very hungry. Do you mind if I go on up and finish getting ready?"

"But Cassie! You have to eat," her mother argued.

"No, she doesn't," Barbara said, pushing her chair back. "You haven't seen the dress she's wearing tonight. A fraction of an inch on that waistline and she won't be able to zip it up!"

"Barbara!"

"Well, it's the truth. I'd have to diet for a month to get into that thing. Come on, I'll help you."

Barbara's devotion to the cause added to Cassie's anticipation, and her sister refused to let a thought apart from Sly cloud her mind. When they were back in Barbara's room, she began taking the rollers out. "I can't wait to see his face. Mom and Dad are going to be scratching their heads and wondering if they missed something. I'm so glad you told me, Cassie. I was upset at first. But one of the highlights of my childhood was watching you two fall in love. And now I get to do it again!''

"Nothing may come of it," Cassie said softly as the shiny auburn curls fell around her face. "Amanda is still in the picture.''

"Well, it won't be because we didn't try," Barbara said, brushing out the curls.

When Barbara had done all she could, she left Cassie alone to gather her wits before Sly arrived. Standing in front of the full-length mirror on Barbara's closet door, she studied her image, trying to see herself from Sly's point of view. Her strapless dress was an original she had found on a buying trip in Paris, and she had spent a fortune on it, not knowing where she would ever wear it. The ivory fabric was soft and clingy, and it draped provocatively over her full breasts. The gathering on one side of the waist pulled the dress tight around her flat stomach, and the knee-length, uneven skirt was slit to the gathering at the upper thigh in a cascade of ruffles, giving the illusion that nothing held it together at all.

Her hair was pulled back in a French twist, and a string of pearls with matching pearl earrings added the finishing touch. Turning from the mirror, she found her purse and hunted for the vial she had brought of her favorite perfume. She touched the scent to the base of her ears and on each wrist, and finally added a dot to the cleavage that hinted at the bare breasts underneath.

A car engine sounded in the gravel driveway outside, and holding her breath, she went to the window and peered out. Sly was getting out of the car,

straightening his black dinner jacket, looking hesitantly toward the house.

Taking a deep breath, Cassie hurried out of the
bedroom and into the living room where her family
was assembled. "I'll get it," she said, eyeing Barbara, who looked as nervous as she.

It wasn't until then that the doorbell rang. Taking
another nervous breath that she hoped her family
didn't notice, she opened the door.

Their eyes met first, then swept the length of each
other's body. Sly was at his best. His custom-tailored
coat was pulled back above his wrists, revealing the
white shirt that darkened his tan and deepened the
blue of his eyes.

"Wow," he breathed out. His smile wavered and his
eyes darted to the family standing behind her. "That
dress didn't look that way on the hanger." The expla-
nation seemed as necessary to her as it did to him, for
only Barbara would understand their enchanted scrutiny of each other.

"Are you ready?" she asked, getting her purse.

"Absolutely," he said, his eyes following her across
the room and back.

After the necessary good-byes, Sly closed the front
door behind them and escorted Cassie to the car, his
hand pressed in the small of her back. He opened her
door, but just before she leaned to get in, he caught
her arm and lifted her chin to him. "You look so
beautiful," he said softly, the evening dusk darkening his features. His lips parted and hovered over hers
until hers opened, too. His kiss was gentle, inspiring
more, promising later. When he pulled back, he
smoothed a hand across the side of her hair. "Don't

dance with anyone else tonight. Just for tonight, let it be the two of us.''

Mesmerized by his voice and the warmth of his arms, Cassie nodded silently. He helped her into the car, then slipped behind the steering wheel. The drive to the Langston Inn, in whose ballroom the party was to take place, was fraught with an eloquent silence that added to the fantasy Cassie was finally letting herself live.

Chapter Nine

If anyone in the class of one hundred fifty graduates had missed the picnic that day, they did not miss the dance. Class members and spouses or dates lined up at the ballroom entrance to register and get their name tags bearing their senior yearbook pictures. Neil Diamond's recorded voice rang from the candlelit room bordered with white-clothed tables, and those who had already gone in made their way out again, drinks in hand, to find old friends and catch up on fifteen years.

Cassie and Sly lost their tension as friends they had not already seen embraced them or slapped them on the backs, tossing comments back and forth about the horrendous pictures they each wore. The camaraderie with old friends drew Cassie closer to Sly, for he had always been beside her when these people had been part of her life. They joked and teased one another, but Sly stayed close to Cassie at all times.

When Blair whisked Cassie off to the ladies' room, Sly winked and told her he'd wait.

"You look great," Blair said when they got into the quieter room. "Where on earth did you find that dress?"

"It's just a little something I picked up in Paris," Cassie teased. "Now, what was it you were dying to tell me?"

Blair's wry smile spread to her eyes. "You'll never guess who brought me here tonight."

"Who?"

"D.H. He called this afternoon and asked if I'd be his date. I said, 'Why not,' you know? I thought, maybe I can do Cassie and Sly a favor and divert his attention a bit."

"You're just the one to do it." Cassie laughed. "Although I'm not sure his attentions need to be 'diverted.' He's always been just as entranced with you as he was with me. But I think Sly will be relieved."

"Sit with us, will you?" Blair asked her. "I have to admit, I'm a little nervous."

"Nervous? The unflappable Blair Callahue? You've got to be kidding."

"Not kidding," Blair said frankly. "Everyone looks different in their best clothes. They're very intimidating."

"Well, you never would have gotten any of us in these back in school," Cassie said.

"Bunch of hypocrites," Blair muttered, running a brush through her platinum hair. "In school we impressed each other by being cool and not worrying about how we looked. But tonight everyone is dressed to the hilt, as if that's our only measure of our success. Wonder how many people hocked their families to look good here tonight.''

Cassie saw the distaste breaking through the pleasant expression on Blair's face. ''Blair, is that bitterness I hear? What's wrong?''

''This,'' she said, pointing to the reunion booklet they'd been given at registration. Opening it to the page that summarized her life, she read, ''Blair Callahue is the divorced mother of an eight-year-old daughter. Her hobbies are needlepoint, tennis, and aerobics. She makes her home in Anaheim, California.'' She dropped the book on the vanity and looked at Cassie, as if the cause for her chagrin were obvious.

''What's wrong with that?''

''It's true. That's what's wrong with it. It's dull and boring and true.'' Blair picked the book back up and flipped to another page. ''They didn't tell me I could lie! Get this one about Paul Landrum. We all know he's one of the best contractors in this city, right? His reads, 'Paul attended Oxford University after graduation, where he studied medicine. He is now a practicing neurosurgeon. His wife, Shelly, an ex-Dallas Cowboy cheerleader, is a star of stage and screen and works nights as a sex therapist.' ''

Despite the forlorn look on Blair's face, Cassie couldn't help laughing at the outrageous story of the class clown.

''They sent that stupid questionnaire, and I told the truth on it. I could have lied or made a joke out of it like Paul did. But I thought I had to tell the truth!''

''What difference does it make?''

"It's just that in school I thought I'd never have to worry about being inferior to these people. I thought we all had the same values. But walking in here tonight, I feel like I don't belong. You and Sly are the only ones who aren't trying to be something you're not."

Cassie dropped her eyes to the purse in her hand, where her fingers had absently been tearing at a sequin. She pressed it back on, wishing Blair hadn't illustrated the hypocrisy so bluntly. If she only knew...

"Well, back to the trenches," Blair said, taking a deep breath. "I knew I should have gone to college."

"You hated school," Cassie reminded her. "You said it inhibited your creative energy and stifled your individuality."

"And it made me feel stupid, too. Did I ever mention that?"

Smiling and shaking her head, Cassie hugged Blair. "Hang in there, kid. There are about sixty working women out there who would give the world to be in your place."

"Divorced?" Blair asked, cocking a brow.

"And financially stable enough to do as you please."

"I wonder," Blair said absently as they pushed through the doors and into the corridor.

"And what are you two lovely ladies talking about?" Sly asked, slipping up from behind them and setting an arm on each of their shoulders.

Cassie smiled at his charming mood. "Blair doesn't feel that she's where she expected to be by the time we had this reunion."

Blair's eyebrows arched at Sly, and he rose to the occasion.

"You didn't expect to be one of the two most gorgeous women at your class reunion? The only one, I might add, who is available?"

A slow grin spread across Blair's lips and to her eyes. "What's the use, Sly," she asked with a teasing wink, "when the most gorgeous man here is already taken?"

"Could you mean me?" Sly asked. "What can I say? Cassie had her choice and she chose the best. Kid always did have class." Cassie grinned at the bantering, but her heart felt heavy for hiding the truth from Blair.

When Blair spotted D.H. across the room, she left them alone. Hooking a possessive hand around Cassie's waist, Sly pulled her toward the doors to the ballroom. "Stay close, Cass," he said in an intimate, husky rumble against her ear as they walked. "You're the sexiest thing here tonight. That dress takes the imagination by the ear and leads it down all kinds of forbidden paths."

Cassie stopped midstride and turned to face Sly. "It doesn't reveal that much. If I'd known you didn't like it—"

"I like it," he whispered, his hands following the curve of her waist. "Guess I just want to believe you wore it for me, and not for these other jerks who can't keep their eyes off you."

Cassie swallowed with great effort, and her heart failed to keep its stable rhythm. "I did wear it for you," she whispered in answer.

He wet his lips, and his breath against hers seemed ragged and uneven. "Let's dance," he said, finally.

He led her onto the dance floor and pulled her against him, his body swaying to "Colour My World."

"Looks like they dug up all of our favorites," she said, wrapping her trembling arms around his shoulders since both of his were around her waist.

The casual reference to the music did nothing to subdue his attentions. "You smell good," he said, looking down into her eyes. His hand rose to her ear. "I remember all the places you used to put perfume. Here," his voice was soft as his hand slid down her forearm to her wrist, fluttering with her racing pulse, "and here," and then his hand came back down her arm, and a hooked finger stroked her chin and made a subtle journey down the column of her neck, down her chest, and stopping at the top of her dress, "and here."

His own exotic scent was fresh, intoxicating, different than she remembered. She wanted to say something in answer, but her throat constricted and nothing would pass her lips.

His arms tightened their embrace, and the songs changed from "Chicago" to an old Elvis tune. His freshly shaven jaw brushed against her cheek, and he pulled back and looked down at her again. "I meant what I said on the phone today." His face was serious; his eyes were intense.

Cassie's green eyes grew wider, and she wanted to look away but felt she had been captured.

"I do love you, Cassie. I've always loved you."

She dropped her eyes to the knot in his tie, but he used his lips to coax her face back to his. When she was looking at him again, he went on in a deep, seductive voice.

"I've hurt you, and you've hurt me. But we can make up for it. Cass, I have no intention of marrying Amanda."

Cassie caught her breath, tried to speak, faltered. "But...I saw the article last week. Your engagement..."

"It was a ploy, Cass," he said earnestly. "She didn't want me to come here with you, because she knew I had never gotten over you. She thought that announcement would tie me to her and keep me from coming. It didn't work."

Cassie stared up into his face. "But there must have been some discussion of marriage," Cassie said, "or she never would have expected to get away with it."

He nodded. "There was some. I was trying to go on with my life, Cass. But I never could commit myself. I couldn't forget you, no matter what I did."

He drew her closer, his voice soft against her ear as he clung to her. Slowly, the world changed. Colors emerged, blended, circled her. "Why didn't you tell me you weren't going to marry her?" she asked in a whisper.

"I really didn't think you cared until today. You acted like it freed you to go on. Finally got me off your back."

"No," she said, clinging to him as the world seemed to spin faster, bringing deeper problems to the surface.

Sly went on, holding her close as the music played. "Those other women before Amanda...they were substitutes. I was trying to get you out of my system.

It didn't work. Not one of those women came close to purging me of you.''

Her eyes filled with tears, and she dropped her face to his chest. "I . . . I don't want to talk about Amanda or those other women," Cassie said, struggling with the words and the emotion flooding her throat. "I don't even want to know who they were."

"You didn't know them," Sly assured. "I would never have gone that far."

"You went far enough." The statement reeked of bitterness, and she hated it. "But it was your right. We were divorced. I had left you, and that gave you the freedom to—"

He stopped swaying, took her face in his hands. "I thought you had stopped loving me. I thought you just wanted out. If I'd known about your attempt to come back, everything would have changed. Everything. I didn't turn to the others until you had moved to New York. It was stupid, but at the time it seemed the only way to keep my sanity. And the only way to keep from running after you and begging you to come back."

"That wouldn't have worked, either," Cassie admitted. "I needed healing time."

"So did I," he said. "Only I suddenly found myself with nothing, and the wounds were deeper than I was."

She understood profoundly what he meant, for those wounds had never completely healed in her, either. She laid her head on his shoulder as the song finished, accepting the comfort of his hands sliding up her back.

"I want you back, Cass," he whispered hoarsely in her ear, his face cradled against her hair. "That's why

I wanted us to come home together this weekend. I thought I might be able to persuade you . . ."

Cassie's head shot up, and she glared at him for a moment before her eyes softened. A new song began to play, as if matching the changing tone in Cassie's heart.

"Don't be angry," he said. "It was my last chance. Cass, if Laura had lived, we would never have split up."

The way he used the baby's name moved her, but his honest statement brought a new wave of bitterness. "We wouldn't have had any reason to split up. We learned a lot about each other then."

"I'm not sure I learned anything," he said. "I just came out of it with more questions." The song played on, and Cassie buried her face in his lapel to hide her pain. His hand molded itself to the nape of her neck, and his voice persisted. "Somehow you blamed me for the baby's death, didn't you?"

The question was posed so naturally, with such forgiveness, that she found herself unable to answer.

His hand found her chin, and he brought her face to his again. With the calloused pad of his thumb, he wiped her tears, but he did nothing for the half-moons that were welling in his own eyes. He opened his mouth to speak, but the music ended and a drumroll cut him off.

"Is everybody having fun?" a voice said through the PA system. Jerry, the class's vice-president and head of the reunion committee, was answered with a chorus of cheers. "It's time to give out the awards! I'll give out some of my favorites, and then we'll get our illustrious president, Sly Farrell, to give the rest."

Sly took Cassie by the hand and led her to the table where Blair was saving them a seat.

Cassie tried to concentrate on the silly awards being given out, a training bra for "Least Changed," a sex manual for "Newliest Wed," a sperm bank for "Mother Having Most Children in Least Amount of Time." But her eyes kept drifting to Sly, who stared at the podium as if he didn't see a thing. The conversation was not over between them, but she was not at all certain she could take the honesty any further. The tension was suffocating, the emotions strangling. Amidst cheers and boos, Jerry continued.

"The next one is for 'Longest Married Couple.' No one has to guess who that is," he said cheerfully. "It's Sly and Cassie Farrell!"

Cassie caught her breath, and Sly turned back to her, forcing a smile and urging her to do the same. He took her hand and they stood up, made their way between the tables and to the platform.

"Let's face it, folks, it gets a little boring after all those years. So for Cassie we have a little distraction. A Chippendales calendar," Jerry said, presenting her with the calendar with a different male "hunk" on each page, "and for Sly, a gift subscription to *Playboy*." Cassie and Sly managed to exchange a teasing look. "Just for the record, though, from the way these two were dancing just now, I don't know if they're that bored yet. So, Sly, if you want to give up that subscription, I'd be happy to take it off your hands." Everyone laughed when Sly handed over the subscription certificate, and Jerry winked at Cassie. "Cassie says she's holding on to hers. Says she won it fair and square."

Still grinning as if enjoying the teasing immensely, Cassie followed Sly off the platform, wanting only to run out of the room and escape the tension between them and the lie that now the whole class was participating in. Sly grabbed her arm to stop her, but Jerry's amplified voice said, "Hold on, Sly. It's your turn to give some of these awards out. Seems like I'm supposed to get the one for 'Most Handsome,' or something, so you take over."

Reluctantly, Sly let Cassie go and went to the podium, his troubled eyes following her as she ran from the room.

It seemed there was no place private enough for Cassie to hide and let her tears overtake her. Every corner was filled with people, and even the rest room was occupied. Dropping the calendar in a trash can and dashing down the stairs that led to the lobby, Cassie decided to step outside, hoping for the anonymity of darkness.

The air was hot and humid outside, but the peace was comforting. Standing against the side of the building, she wept into her hands. She was not a rock, as Sasha and Sly seemed to think before they'd seen her melt into tears at the drop of a hat this weekend. She certainly had not gone through life never shedding a tear. But even as a child, she had only cried in total privacy. She had exercised complete control over her emotions when in the company of even those closest to her. She wasn't that strong anymore.

Either that, she thought, or the pains were much too great for her to bear.

Longest Married Couple. The title tied her stomach in knots that rooted her sobs deeper. They had not been the first to marry after high school, but those who had were divorced. Just as she and Sly were divorced.

And what would happen when she faced him again, after their conversation had ended with such an explosive question? How would she react? He would certainly want her to elaborate on any answer she gave him.

Cassie dug through her purse for a tissue and dabbed at her face to dry the tears. There was no telling what shape her makeup was in now, she thought, and if she went into the bathroom, the gossip would begin immediately when the others saw that she was crying. Maybe she could find one in the lobby, she thought dismally. Maybe she could get to one without anyone seeing her.

She started around the building to the front doors, but stopped when she saw Sly coming out.

"Where have you been?" he asked in a rush, taking her in his arms. "I've been looking all over for you."

"I needed some air," she said.

He looked down at her averted eyes, and a deep frown cleaved his forehead. "You need more than that, I think," he said, holding her close as he opened the door and escorted her back into the lobby. "We both need to talk, and I've seen enough of the old gang for a while. How about if I find a place where we can be alone?"

The tears were beginning to flow again, despite her efforts to stop them. Passively, she nodded. Keeping her head bowed so that no one could see her face, she went with him to the registration desk of the hotel. "I believe I have a reservation for Mr. and Mrs. Sly Farrell," he told the clerk.

Cassie's face came up, and Sly grinned down at her. "I forgot to cancel," he said with a shrug.

When he'd gotten the key, he took her in the elevator to the designated floor, found the room, and let them in.

His eyes were serious when he flicked on the lamp and turned back to her. Taking her hands, he sat down on the edge of the bed and pulled her onto his lap. "I love you, Cassie. I want you to talk to me."

New tears squeezed out of her closed eyes, and she buried her face in his collar. "I just can't take much more. I didn't expect it to be like this."

"It doesn't have to be," he said. "It can be a new beginning. We just have to talk it out."

"Talking won't change things," she said, pulling away from him and sliding to the head of the bed where she leaned back against the pillow.

"It might," he said, inching closer to her and facing her on the bed. "You never answered my question, Cass. I have to know, if not to rebuild our relationship, then to rebuild my own sanity." His voice was soft, pleading. "Did you blame me for the baby's death?"

Cassie covered her face with shaking hands. "No. Not for the death. For after it."

"After it? Why?"

Pinching the bridge of her nose, she said, "I shouldn't have blamed you. You reacted the way you felt."

"*How* did I react, Cass? Honest to God, those days seem to be such a blur that I don't remember."

Cassie couldn't hold back the hostility and misery washing over her. "Like you didn't care. Like it didn't matter. You were happy, and cheerful, and—"

"Like hell I was!" Trembling hands took Cassie by the shoulders. "Is that what you thought? You thought I didn't care that the baby I'd been anticipating for years was stillborn? You thought I forgot about it just like that?"

Cassie swallowed and looked him in the eye. "The next morning, you told me that you'd packed up all the baby's things. You said you were giving them away. You even said it must have been for the best that she died. And you told me that now I wouldn't have to quit working, that I could concentrate on my career, as if that would comfort me."

Sly's mouth opened, and his face contorted as he struggled to remember that day. "Cass, I was worried about you. I was trying to cheer you up. I put on that facade when I went into your room, thinking that the last thing you needed was to see my pain."

"What pain?" Cassie cried as months of agony surfaced. "You never suffered any pain. You didn't even go home the night she was born. You went to a bar and got drunk!"

"I did what? What are you talking about?"

"I'm talking about when I called home that night after you left the hospital. I needed to talk to you, and you weren't home all night. The next day when you got there you looked like hell, and you told me that you had a hangover. A hangover! Our baby had died, and the only pain you had was a hangover."

Anger twisted Sly's face, and he jumped up, grabbed an ashtray, and threw it at the wall where it shattered into a million pieces. Turning back to Cassie, he looked almost dangerous, as if he would send her flying next. "You want to know what I did that night? I went home and the phone was ringing. I thought it was your mother or someone calling to see how you were, so I ripped the phone cords out of the walls. I went in the baby's room and saw how carefully you had prepared everything before you went to the hospital, and the instruction sheet you had left me. People I was supposed to call, things I was supposed to buy for the homecoming. You had even laid out the pink and blue outfits on the crib side, and I was supposed to bring the right one to the hospital after the baby was born. Only I knew that if we took the doctor's advice and had a funeral, our child would wear that homecoming dress to her grave! I didn't go to a bar that night, Cass. I sat down in the rocking chair in the baby's room and cried until I was sick. And then I packed up everything and put it away so you would be spared that added suffering when you got home!"

Cassie felt the world she'd known for over a year slipping from under her. Slowly, she saw her reality becoming a lie, and the lie becoming truth.

Sly covered his face with both hands, then dropped them to his sides. "I told you I had a hangover because I didn't want you to know how torn up I was. I was terrified that you'd somehow blame yourself for the stillbirth. I know you, Cass. I know how you think. So I tried to distract you. You never cried. You never showed any pain. But from the moment we knew the baby was dead, no one could reach you. You built a wall around yourself, and I thought I just had to give you time, let you deal with it in your own way, that you would turn to me when you were ready. But the next thing I knew you were flying off to Mexico for a quick divorce and moving your things to New York. And I just didn't know how to fight that.''

It seemed as if Cassie were seeing her life played before her on a gigantic screen, all her mistakes and misconceptions in living color. ''I needed you, Sly,'' she whispered. ''But I didn't think I could share that grief with you when you didn't feel it. I thought—''

Sly's anger drained from his face, and his eyes grew moist. He sat facing Cassie on the bed. ''Baby, you thought wrong. I suffered. Twice as much as was necessary, because I lost you, too. I wound up with nothing.'' He studied her face, as if it held answers to the complicated past. ''We were selfish with our grief. Maybe I would have reached out more if I hadn't been so caught up in my own pain. Maybe you would have turned to me if I'd let myself be more human, more accessible.''

''You worked twice as many hours after that; you never mentioned the baby...''

Sly nodded. ''It was my own escape. I didn't know any other way to deal with it. I guess you did the only thing you knew to do, too. But it was all wrong, Cass. Don't you see?''

Cassie pulled herself off the bed and went to the window where she could see Langston's downtown streets threaded with late night traffic. ''I saw that possibility later, when I decided to come back to you. But when you were with another woman already, I thought I had never really known you at all.''

Sly stood up and slid his arms around her waist, his eyes penetrating her very soul. ''I didn't know myself, Cass. I just wanted not to think, not to feel, so I made a mockery out of every feeling I had. I wanted you. All I ever wanted was you."

"We've wasted so much," she whispered as new hope rose in her heart.

"We can get it back," he promised.

Their eyes embraced for a long, revealing moment, and Cassie knew that the love she saw in those cerulean depths was the only truth that mattered. As his lips lowered to hers, their souls reuniting in bold defiance of the lies that had kept them apart, Cassie knew that her reality had been nothing more than a poorly constructed illusion.

For there was no reality without Sly.

Chapter Ten

Sly's hands gently molded Cassie's face, and his lips made a startling entreaty that she had no power to deny. His mouth opened and closed upon hers, tasting, savoring, then nipping, and his fingers went to the pins in her hair and worked them free, pulling the auburn strands until they tumbled around her shoulders in deep waves.

"I won't let you leave me again," he warned against her lips, brushing his fingers into the silky mass of her hair. "I'll make you want to stay."

When he kissed her again with greater depth and stronger demand, she felt his silken net capturing her heart as he had captured it long ago, but it was a welcome prison. She had no desire to pull it free again, for it was only in his love that she found strength to deal with the past.

His hand glided across her bare shoulder, down her arm, back up to the swell of breast where her dress curved low. Cassie slipped his tie out of its knot, pulling it off his neck to drop onto the floor, then opened the top button of his shirt and kissed the hollow of his throat, feeling the vibration of his moan against her lips as her fingers freed each button. Her lips followed the opening, from the thick mass of hair across his warm chest to the thinner line brushing down the center of his stomach. Her lips trailed up his ribs as she pulled his shirt open and found one dark nipple, then sucked at its peak as she worked the shirt off his shoulders.

Pulling her face back to his, Sly kissed her deeply, his hands finding the opening in her dress at the thigh, sliding beneath it to mold the smooth skin of her hips, crushing her desperately against him. His tongue thrust against hers in the rhythm set by her hips, and she broke free of his lips to catch her breath. His lips moved to her throat, biting and feathering while his hands, trembling with control, made the upward curve from her waist and found her breasts, swelling and straining against the soft fabric that covered them. He found the zipper at her side and pulled it down, peeling the cloth away from her flushing skin, his blue eyes glittering at the swollen mounds of aroused femininity.

When her dress dropped to the floor, he slid his hands into the lacy scrap of bikini, kneading her with the rhythm of his heart as her breasts crushed into his chest. With short, heavy breaths, she slipped her hands between them and unbuckled his belt, freed the button at his waist, and pushed down the zipper, while the

pressure caused his stomach to constrict with re-
straint. He worked her panties over her hips, his kiss
journeying down her neck, over her breasts, and down
the soft plane of her stomach while he pulled the nylon triangle off her legs.

Stooping before her, he looked up at her for a long
moment, exploring every dip and curve and point of
her slim body, his hooded eyes the smoky-blue color
of twilight. His gentle hands closed around her calves
and slid slowly up the back of her body, until he stood
before her again. Soft black lashes brushed against her
face as his lips claimed hers again, and he lowered her
onto the bed, kicked out of his own clothes, and anchored her with his hard weight.

Without entering her, his body moved against her,
teasing close to the point of mania, always stopping
short of consumation. With her eyes shut tight, she
breathed in gasps and moaned when he took her to
horizon's boundary and drew her back to make the
voyage again.

When her body quivered with the fierce strength of
desire, he entered her slowly, gaining momentum as
she fed the fury of his mounting passion. Moans min-
gled and their bodies glistened in the yellow lamp-
light. Swift bursts of ecstasy blinded her, each one
more devastating than the others, until the final tor-
rent drenched her with the power of a hailstorm in all
its fury.

The glorious aftermath was the sealing factor of
their renewed commitment, for while their bodies were
yet linked, still throbbing with the warmth of ardor,
he looked into the luminous glow of her eyes. "Marry
me again, Cass," he whispered. "Start over with me."

Her surrendering kiss was answer enough to bring new life to his body, swelling inside hers as fresh, melding desire surged through them again. As if it had not just happened, he made love to her again, with slow, gentle motions born of deep love and fresh commitment.

When their passion was spent, they slept like trusting children in each other's arms, then woke as the promise of morning painted the room in pink-orange hues.

"I made you miss the reunion," Cassie whispered when she woke to his smiling, pensive eyes.

"I didn't come back here for the reunion," he told her, lifting a strand of her hair and stroking it between two fingers. "I came back for you. The reunion was just an excuse."

Cassie smiled. "Did you plan to get me in this hotel room all along? Is that why you never cancelled the reservations?"

Sly grinned sheepishly. "You didn't actually think I'd let this whole weekend pass without one night absolutely alone with you, did you? I called yesterday to make sure we still had the room."

Cassie rolled onto her back and stretched like a cat. "I should have known. And you probably never had any intention of getting a two-bedroom suite."

"None whatsoever." Laughing, he gathered her against him. "Come take a shower with me, you little nymph. I'm so enchanted with this ripe body," he said, feathering his tongue across a nipple and stirring new desires in her, "that I can't stand to part with it for five minutes."

"I'm at your mercy," she teased in a hoarse voice, knowing and loving the power she had over him as much as she loved his own power.

He picked her up then, and carried her to the shower where he set her down. As the water pounded over them, he lathered and rinsed her, his hands and lips following the paths of the water over her body. She played him with intimate knowledge of his sensitive spots, and when they came together, water spraying like rain over them, she knew there could never be another morning shower without the thought of Sly. In a weekend's time he had invaded every secret chamber of her heart, filling it with a dazzling light greater than any she'd ever known.

As they dried each other, Sly's question came again. "Will you marry me, Cass? Give us another chance. Start over with me."

His eyes, blue as a clear morning sky, stopped her heart and told her it would never beat again without the hard, steady rhythm of his own.

"Yes," she whispered, "I'll marry you again."

His eyes became two round sapphires glistening with the mist of joy and relief. He threw his arms around her and lifted her, swinging her around. "She's going to marry me," he exclaimed, then in a louder, more exulting voice, "She's going to marry me!"

Setting her down, he ran for the phone and dialed one digit. "Send champagne to 619," he said. "Oh, and two omelets, I guess. My wife is going to marry me!" He lifted her again when she laughed aloud, and they fell onto the bed, necking like adolescent lovers with no guarantees that the chance would come again. Then they dressed in the clothes of the night before and let in room service, to whom Sly tipped an exorbitant amount for simply being there to share the news.

Cassie felt an unprecedented joy as they drank champagne and ate their omelets, making plans for the wedding they wanted to take place as soon as possible, and toasting the future and their new life together.

"The only problem with the fact that we never told anyone here we were divorced," Sly said, "is that we can't tell them we're getting remarried. I want to tell the world!" He rose from the table and went to Cassie, pulled her up and sat in her chair, pulling her back onto his lap. "It'll be better this time, Cass. You'll see. No more mistakes. No more disappointments. And we can start trying to have a family again. I need a family. I need a houseful of happy voices to come home to. A man isn't complete without his own children. Cass, you and I will finally have that family."

Cassie's smile ebbed, and suddenly the champagne in her mouth turned sour. She felt the anxiety of trying for years to conceive; the fear that the doctors were wrong when they pronounced her fertility problems resolved; the elation of pregnancy, followed by the ache of hard labor in her lower back. She heard the nurses scurrying around when the monitor showed that the baby's heartbeat had ceased, felt Sly blotting beads of perspiration from her brow. And then came the final push, the feeling of tremendous relief, and the horrible, heartrending silence. No merciful warning. No comfort that it had been for the best. No answers. Only the dead silence of nurses taking the

lifeless body away, and the doctor's brutal announcement that there was nothing he could do.

Slowly, Cassie pulled herself off Sly's lap and went
to the dresser, opened her purse, and pulled out a
hairbrush, the first thing her hand touched.

"I'll go to New York with you today, and we'll pack
your things. Do you think you could take time off for
a honeymoon? We could go on a cruise, or we could
spend some time in Europe, or we could just hole up
at home and not answer the phone or the door for a
couple of weeks."

A man isn't complete without his own children. The
words deafened her to the rest of Sly's ramblings. She
stared at the bristles on the brush, but nothing reached
her mind except for the miserable, frightening thought
of pregnancy. *Pregnancy.* Nine months of hope that
end in nine hours of pain. Nine months of anticipation, excitement. Nine months that result in misery
and tragedy. Never again would Cassie have the
strength to invest herself or her emotions in a pregnancy. Never again. She had pushed too hard, or she
hadn't pushed hard enough, or she should have accepted anesthesia to make it easier on the baby, or...
A difficult birth, the doctor had said. These things
happened.

"Cass? Did I say something wrong?" Sly was behind her now, his hands on her hips, looking over her
shoulder at her pale image in the mirror.

Cassie swallowed and tried to keep her voice steady
as the barriers Sly had broken down overnight re-
emerged around her. "It's just...I don't know if I can
move that quickly. I have my job, and..."

"You worked from Chicago before. Can't you just move your office back to the Chicago store?"

She couldn't meet his eyes. "They've gotten used to having me in New York." Her statement had a dull note of finality.

The pressure of his hands on her hips tightened. He kept his voice low, calm. "Most of my clients are in Chicago. It wouldn't be feasible for me to move my business—"

"Of course not. You can't move. But my home store is in New York. It'll take time to settle things there."

"How much time?"

Cassie pulled away from him and went to look out the window. "A few months. I'm not sure—"

"Months! Cass, you told me you'd marry me. We've wasted a whole year. What's more important here?"

Her hands were suddenly trembling at her side and her legs became weak. Lowering onto the bed, she dropped her head. Sly was more important, but he wanted children, and she couldn't—wouldn't—give them. If she told him, he would only launch a campaign to convince her otherwise. It was a point on which she could not negotiate. There was no use discussing it. The thought nearly sent her into hysterics. If she told him . . .

"Cass, answer me! Are you going to marry me or not?"

She couldn't answer. It wasn't a simple yes or no question. It was filled with conditions that couldn't be met, couldn't be faced. She could feel Sly's anger and pain rising like a solid wall they would never have the heart to cross over again. She wanted to reach out to him, share her fears. But too much was at stake. Her sanity hinged on avoiding what she feared at any cost.

"So," he said after several moments of silence. "I guess that's your answer. Just like that, you changed your mind." He stared at her for a moment, then straightened and turned back to the dresser. Slowly, mechanically, Sly gathered his wallet and keys and the loose change that was lying there. He turned back to Cassie, his unshaven face taut and expressionless. He handed Cassie her purse. "Come on," he said in a flat, wooden monotone. "We both have a plane to catch. We'll have to go back to my parents' house and pack."

And without exchanging another word, they left the room where their new commitment to each other had slipped through their fingers like pieces of shattered crystal that they had tried to glue back together, but failed.

Breakfast was over in the Farrell household when Cassie and Sly came home, and Sasha greeted them at the door, a hopeful glimmer in her gray eyes. "Long party?" she asked playfully.

Sly shrugged and pushed past his grandmother. "It was over late, so we just took a hotel room there so we wouldn't wake everyone when we came home."

"Oh?" The enthusiasm in Sasha's voice began to wane at Sly's coarseness, and she turned to Cassie, her face trembling slightly. "I thought maybe..."

Cassie averted her eyes to avoid the honest question in Sasha's. "I hope we didn't worry you."

"Excuse me," Sly said, starting up the stairs. "Our plane leaves in a couple of hours, so I have to go up and pack."

Sasha turned back to Cassie, feisty anger in her eyes forewarning the lecture she was about to embark on. "What is the matter with you two?"

Cassie swallowed the lump of tears in her throat and started up the stairs. "I have to pack, too," she choked, but Sasha stopped her flight with a thin, palsied hand.

"Look me in the eye, Cassandra Farrell," she ordered in her hoarse, angry voice. "And tell me if I have something to worry about."

"Nothing," Cassie said, wishing she could do more to set Sasha's fears to rest. "We talked, like you wanted. There's nothing to worry about." She knew the dismal note in her voice belied her assurance.

Sasha's body wavered, and she grabbed onto the banister. "Go help your husband pack," she said in a weary voice. "I'll be down here when you're finished."

Cassie hurried up the stairs and went into the room, still decorated exclusively for them, its beauty and promise a cruel mockery of a marriage that had died. Sly's suitcase was open on the bed, and she heard him in the bathroom tossing items into his shaving kit. She went to the dresser where his cologne sat, lifted it to her nose and inhaled the fresh, exotic scent that reminded her of last night. His tie lay in a crumpled heap where he had dropped it, and his monogrammed clasp rested on its side, along with his silver cuff links. Beside them were a few pennies, a dime, two nickels—and in the center of the loose change he had set his wedding ring. Cassie clenched her left hand into a fist and looked at her own simple band. Once again she would take it off and say good-bye to the past. No matter how dismal the future seemed. With trembling fingers, she pulled off the ring and set it next to Sly's. She hoped Amanda could make him happy. She hoped that she was a woman whose fears did not dictate her life. Someone strong enough to live up to his image of her and give him those children he said he needed.

When Sly came out, she saw that he had changed into a pair of worn jeans and a denim shirt with the sleeves rolled up. His tousled black hair reflected the stark confusion in his eyes. He dropped his shaving kit into his suitcase, gathered the last of his belongings, and slammed it shut. "The bathroom's all yours," he mumbled.

Taking a pair of jeans and a shirt of her own, Cassie went into the bathroom and dressed, then came out and dropped her evening dress into her suitcase in a heap. She'd never wear it again, she decided, for it would always remind her of life's greatest disappointments. The promises that had been dangled before her nose with a condition attached. She found her stray belongings—hairbrush, makeup and shampoo—and packed them. "I forgot to check on my lost bag," she said, though it didn't make any difference anymore.

"You can do it at the airport," Sly said.

Cassie sat on the bed and looked at him, bending over his suitcase as wearily as if he'd just come out of a battle zone where he'd almost lost his life. But the war was not over, his eyes seemed to say as they fixed on the gray shell of his suitcase. There were memories to bury, and many more battles to fight before peace would come again. Cassie could see that she had hurt him deeply by holding back, but she wasn't able to change things. Life held pure, simple, cruel facts that hit people at the worst times, stealing all hope of happiness. If only she could make him see that she hadn't changed her mind about *him*. "Sly, I—"

"Don't!" he shouted, startling her. "I don't want to hear it. You're not worried about relocating your office. We both know it could be worked out, if you cared enough. But you can't force yourself to care, Cass. Forget everything I said to you this weekend. Forget I asked you to marry me. I don't want to marry you anymore. There has to be some kind of end to this pain."

Cassie couldn't bear much more. Was the agony of hurting Sly as great as the fear of another pregnancy? They were equally threatening, she thought. Biting her lip, she started toward him, but he shook off her arms and went to the bedroom door. "It's time we ended this once and for all." He opened the door and started down the hall, his face reddening by degrees.

"Sly! What are you going to do?"

He turned back to her a moment, his eyes two burning, stinging gems that scorched her heart. "I'm going to tell the truth, Cass. I'm going to put us both out of our misery."

Catching her breath, Cassie ran after him, but before she could stop him he had bolted into the kitchen and was standing like an executioner before both of his parents and Sasha. "Sly, don't. Please don't!" she cried, but it was too late.

"Sit down, Cass," he said in a quiet, controlled voice. "It's time we faced the truth."

"What truth?" Sasha clipped impatiently.

Sly studied his grandmother, took a deep breath, glanced at Cassie. "We were worried about your health, Grandma. We didn't want to disappoint you."

Sasha slammed a flat palm on the kitchen table. "By God, Sly, I know something's wrong! Just spit it out!"

Sly leaned on the table with both hands, dropping his head. His voice was barely audible when he spoke. "Cass and I split up a year ago. After the baby died. We're not married anymore, Grandma. We're divorced."

Sasha's hand went to her mouth, and Sly's father sprang out of his seat, clutching his wife's hand. "What the hell are you talking about?" he bellowed, turning to Cassie for confirmation.

"It's true, Jasper," she said, biting the tremor in her lips. "We didn't want you to know, so we pretended we were still married. Just for the weekend."

"But you...you still love each other!" Sasha shouted. "I'm not blind. You two still care for each other. We all make mistakes, but that doesn't mean they can't be erased!"

"I'm sorry, Grandma," Sly said with eyes so sad that Cassie knew they would haunt her dreams for the rest of her life. "It's over with Cass and me. The sooner we all face it, the sooner we can get back to our lives." His sharp words caused Cassie's face to twist with pain, and she covered it with her hands.

"I can't believe this." Sly's mother bit out the words. "What was the point in keeping it from us all this time?"

"It was too soon after Grandma's heart attack," Sly said quietly. "We wanted to wait until she was stronger."

"Nonsense!" Sasha blurted. "If you kept it a secret it was because *you* couldn't deal with it. Not because of me. If you lied about it, maybe it wouldn't be real. Well, it's real now. Do you both feel better?"

Sly's moist eyes met Cassie's, and they both looked back at Sasha. "No, Sasha," Cassie said. "Would you have preferred that we kept on lying about it?"

"Yes!" Sasha exclaimed. "If it got you back together for a while, yes! Sometimes the truth is just disguised as a lie. Whatever it takes to make you see is what I want for you." Her face shook harder than usual, and she slammed her hand on the table again. "You buried the baby and all your dreams with it. Is that fair? To give up on everything just because of one disappointment?"

Sly brought his eyes back to Cassie, waiting for her answer.

"That's not what we're doing, Sasha," she choked, wiping away her tears.

Sasha shoved back her chair, pulled herself up, and started for the kitchen door. "If you can't be honest with yourselves, then don't even talk to me. I don't want to listen to any more of this nonsense."

Together, they watched her disappear through the swinging door, and found that the silence she left in her wake was more painful than had been the final admission. Sly's parents asked a multitude of ques-

tions before they suggested that Cassie's parents be
told immediately. Since Cassie had no heart to face
Barbara with the new failure, she called and asked her
parents to come over alone, and told them of the divorce at the Farrell's house.

When the tears and anger were spent and there was
nothing more to say, Cassie and Sly said their good-
byes and got Sly's father to drive them to the airport.
Silence seemed a lethal chemical mixed with the air
that threatened to strangle Cassie, but there was no
turning back. She had hurt Sly by turning in upon
herself, and he had hurt her by needing more than she
could give.

They sat next to each other on the flight to Atlanta,
but they couldn't have been farther apart. Sly seemed
to sleep all the way home, and Cassie stared out the
window, wondering how she would endure the dark
emptiness of her apartment, continuing as if her life-
blood didn't warm to Sly's smile.

When they reached the Atlanta airport, they stood
in the wide corridor as hordes of people rushed past
them with joys and pains, lies and truths of their own.
Sly only looked into her eyes, and Cassie couldn't
think of anything appropriate to say. She wanted to
shout, *Take me as I am. I love you, but I haven't finished healing, yet.* The words seemed absurd, and she
had long ago lost the strength to say them.

"Let's not be complete strangers," Sly said quietly,
his eyes open wide as if the act of blinking would
shatter them. "If you're ever in Chicago—"

"I'll call," she choked out through tear-blurred
eyes. "Sly—"

He touched a finger to her lips and breathed, "Shh. It's all been said. Let's just go home like two mature adults who couldn't find their way back together. People do it all the time. There must be some way to learn to deal with it."

Cassie swallowed and nodded. More tears, coming from deeper in her heart, welled in her eyes. "It's late. I'd better go," she responded, choking on the words, then reached up to kiss him before she hurried off to her gate, leaving him staring wistfully after her.

Chapter Eleven

Sly's face followed her home to haunt her in her sleep, in the faces of crowds she found herself in, in the people she encountered at work. She could not escape it, the feel of his arms, or the whispered promises he'd made to her before everything fell apart.

It was Saturday, a rainy day in New York, only a week after she'd left him. She had brought her work home with her for something to do, and was absently comparing colors and textures when the doorbell rang. As it had done for the past week when the possibility arose, her heart lurched with the hope that it would be Sly.

"Hello, beautiful," Frank said when she answered it.

Her heart sank as she smiled at the man who always brought her tidings of Sly when he was in town on business. "Frank. I didn't know you were in town."

"Came straight here from the airport," he said. "I didn't have to be here until Monday, but I thought we could do the town tonight."

Cassie sighed and let him in, watching as he plopped onto the couch. His hair, blond and immaculately styled, had been cut recently, exposing an inch of untanned forehead. "Not tonight, Frank," she said. "I'm not in the mood."

Frank laughed. "Yeah. I guess last weekend kind of took it out of you."

Cassie frowned and sat down on the chair across from him. "What do you know about last weekend?"

"Enough," he said. "That you and Sly nearly got back together until you thought better of it."

Cassie was stunned that Sly would have shared their intimate moments so openly. "I can't believe he told you that," she said in a low voice.

"Oh, *he* didn't tell me. I can't get anything out of him. Amanda told me. Seems he confessed the whole weekend to her and begged her forgiveness. They've set a date now, you know. Next month, I think."

Cassie felt the blood rushing from her face, stealing warmth and life from her. "No. I...I didn't know."

Frank got up and moved to squat in front of her. "I'm sorry, Cassie. I thought you'd have heard. It kind of frees you, though, doesn't it?"

Cassie had singled out a thread in the green carpet she detested. "Frees me?" she asked in a distant voice.

"Well, yeah," he said, cocking a brow. "To move on. To form new attachments."

Cassie didn't answer. Her body swayed, and the carpet blurred. Frank caught her shoulders, slid his hands up her neck, circled her face. "Cass, there are those of us who've been waiting a long time for you to let go of Sly."

Cassie heard the words from far away, and brought her eyes back to Frank.

"I've been waiting for you, Cassie," he said. "I'll help you through this."

His body lifted to meet hers, and he closed his mouth over her lips, prying them open, coaxing a response. But she only pulled away and stood up. "Frank, how could you? You were Sly's friend first. He trusted you."

Frank laughed. "Trusted me? Cassie, I'm not doing anything to hurt him. He's marrying another woman. You two are divorced."

As if it were the first time she'd heard it, the idea frosted her heart. "I...I'm not ready for that kind of relationship, yet. I need time, Frank."

Frank stood up, setting his hands on his hips. "Cassie, how much more time will you take? It's been a year."

Fury raged inside her. "I've been involved with him all my life! I've loved him since I was thirteen! If it takes me twenty years to get over him, I'll take it!"

Frank held his hands out to calm her. "I'm sorry. I didn't mean..."

"I know what you meant," Cassie said dejectedly, going to the door. "I've believed everything you've said all this time because I trusted you. I didn't know you'd been telling Sly all the things I did the way you told me about him. He said you had ulterior motives, but I guess I had to see it for myself. I'm not interested in a relationship with you, Frank, and I'm not interested in any information you get from Amanda. I'll get my facts straight from him from now on, thank you. Now, if you don't mind, I have things to do. Please leave.''

Frank started to speak, then stopped himself. Lifting his chin defiantly, he left her apartment without another word.

Closing the door, Cassie tore a tissue out of its box and pressed it to her eyes, letting new tears soak it. It wasn't true, she told herself. Sly had told her he had no intention of marrying Amanda. Would he have turned back to her that quickly?

Vowing not to take Frank's word for it, Cassie went to the phone and picked it up. The dial tone hummed its dare in her ear, threatening her whether she made the call or hung up. What would she say? That she'd made a mistake? That he was worth the risk of another pregnancy, if that was what he wanted? That it wasn't in her destiny to stop loving him?

Dialing his number, Cassie held her breath. Each ring constricted her heart more, until on the third ring the phone was answered.

"Hello?" The voice was a woman's, soft and sultry against a background of music.

Cassie swallowed. "Is this the Farrell residence?" she asked to be sure.

"Yes," the woman answered. "Who's this?"

"It's Cassie," she said, still undaunted. "I'd like to speak to Sly."

A moment of silence followed, and the woman's voice lowered. "Sly can't come to the phone right now. He's in the shower. What do you want?"

"Just to talk to him," Cassie pressed, letting fresh tears warm her chilled hands.

"I don't think he wants to talk to you," the woman said. "Your little plan failed last weekend, Cassie. He's going to marry me now."

Cassie closed her eyes and cleared her throat. "I still want to talk to him."

"Good luck." The woman clipped the words, hanging up.

Cassie clung to the receiver as the line to Sly was cut off for the last time. He was gone. She would never get him back again.

The Sunday sky was overcast with dark clouds that smothered the light of the sun, the way they had done each day for the two weeks since Cassie had left Langston. If it would only rain, she thought, perhaps she could get on with things, and stop feeling as if she were marking time until the cloudburst that would wash her life clean of the past. A stray ball from a nearby game of catch between a father and son rolled to a stop in front of her. Absently, she picked it up and tossed it toward the grass where the two waited. From the back, the man looked like Sly. Everyone looked like Sly lately, she thought as she started out of the park toward home. She wondered how many months would pass before she'd spend a day without a thought of him.

Work had been a series of mistakes during the past week, for her mind was cluttered with thoughts of Sly married to another woman. She wondered if she should take a long vacation to get back her wits. But the thought of empty time, like the quiet nights or the eternal, lonely weekends, changed her mind.

Where was Sly right now? she wondered. Was he with Amanda? Were they planning a family? Would he bring her to live in the home Cassie had chosen with him? Or did she already live there?

She had done a great deal of thinking since she'd spoken to Amanda. In her office at work, on the train coming home, in the kitchen as she stared into the refrigerator looking for something that would make her stomach feel less queasy. But there seemed to be no solutions, and nothing soothed the misery of losing Sly again.

Turning down the sidewalk that led to her apartment building, Cassie wondered how she would fill the rest of the day. There were drawers that needed cleaning. Closets that needed straightening. She could read a book or watch a movie on television. The possibilities sickened her, and she wished for Monday morning so that she could go to work and start the cycle all over again.

As she approached the underside of the stairwell leading to her second-story apartment, she saw, through the wrought iron steps, the dark form of a man sitting at the foot of the stairs. His head and shoulders were bent in a familiar, dejected slump. Catching her breath, she hurried around the staircase.

"Sly!"

"Hi," he said softly, his eyes brightening at the sight of her. He wore a white pullover shirt and a pair of tight jeans, and he stood up slowly, his eyes failing to reveal his thoughts. "I've been waiting for you. No one knew where you were."

"I was walking. I . . . I didn't expect—"

"It's Sasha," he said quietly, and instantly a surge of panic rose within her.

"What's wrong? She's not . . ." The word wouldn't come, for the act of saying it might have made it true.

"She's in the hospital," he said quickly.

Cassie touched her heart, willing it to ration out its beats. "Another heart attack?"

"I don't think so. All Mom could tell me was that she kept drifting in and out of consciousness. She keeps asking for us. That's why I came here. Mom says there isn't much time." His eyes were grieving, and Cassie couldn't help sliding her arms around him in a silent plea for assurance. He answered by clinging to her. "She's dying, Cass. We have to go to her."

Cassie squeezed her eyes shut, but the tears found a way out. "We did that to her, didn't we? We hurt her."

Sly's arms tightened around her, his hand brushing through her hair, and she heard him swallow against her ear. "She believed in us," he said dismally. "Will you go home with me, Cass? She loves you, too."

"Of course I'll go," Cassie said, reluctantly letting go of him. "Give me ten minutes to go up and get my things together."

Sly had chartered a plane, and they sat aboard it holding hands as if letting go of each other would mean letting go of Sasha. When they landed in Langston they rented a car and drove straight to the hospital where Sasha had been admitted.

The family was assembled in the waiting room, pacing, sitting, waiting for word that Sasha would be all right. Cassie's parents were there, too, standing against the wall, watching helplessly as Sly's mother and father tried to be strong.

"How is she?" Sly asked immediately.

"They think it was a stroke," Jasper told them.

"What are they doing for her?"

Jasper shrugged. "She's had tests. Electrocardiogram, CAT scan, chest X rays. The doctor doesn't seem to be sure about anything."

Sly looked up the hall at the nurses walking in and out of rooms without a hint of urgency. "Why isn't she in intensive care?"

"I don't know," Jasper said, rubbing at the tiredness on his face. "They don't seem to think there's a need. One of us is staying with her all the time, but other than that—"

"She's unconscious," Martha blurted bitterly. "How can they think there's no need?"

"Can we see her?" Cassie asked.

Martha nodded. "Room 402. Tell the nurse who you are."

With arms wrapped around each other for support, Cassie and Sly found the room and pushed open the door. Sly's brother and his wife, who had come from out of town, sat at Sasha's side.

"How's she doing?" Sly asked after they'd exchanged embraces.

"She's breathing normally, and the nurse says her pulse is strong. Blood pressure's a little high, though," his brother said in a quiet voice.

Cassie went to Sasha's bedside and saw the thin, small body that seemed to be lost under the sheets. A tube ran from her nose, and an IV ran into her veins, but her breathing seemed deep and steady, as if she were only sleeping. "Why is she unconscious?"

"They aren't sure."

Sly stepped up behind Cassie, holding her shoulders, resting his head on hers. "She isn't going to die, Cass. She's got to be all right."

Cassie leaned over the rail until her face was close to the old woman's ear. "It's us, Sasha. Cassie and Sly. Can you hear me?" Sasha lay limp, offering no sign that she had heard. Cassie held her breath to stop the onslaught of emotion, but it caught hold of her anyway. "We're sorry we hurt you. We never wanted to." Her voice trailed off, and she clamped a hand over her mouth to quiet her sobs. Sly leaned over his grandmother and kissed her cheek. "We love you, Grandma," he whispered.

When they left the room, they joined the family, still clinging to each other as if their unity had some healing power they didn't have the time to understand.

"You said she asked for us," Sly told his mother when they'd settled on the couch next to her.

Martha nodded. "She's almost come to a couple of times, and she mumbled your names. She hasn't been the same since you told her about your divorce. And this morning she just didn't wake up."

Sly closed his eyes, held Cassie against him, and rested his head on hers.

"Why aren't they *doing* something?" Cassie asked through her teeth. She felt as if her life had gone haywire, and she had no control at all. It was as if she were falling, and she would hit the bottom when Sasha let go.

Jasper stood up and walked to the edge of the waiting area, looked up and down the hall. "They won't know how serious it is until she's conscious."

"What if she doesn't wake up?" The thought rolled from Cassie's tongue without thought, and no one answered.

Finally, Sly stood up. "Let's go get coffee," he told her. He looked at his mother. "We'll bring some back. Let us know if anything . . . happens."

When they were alone in the cafeteria, holding their coffee cups as if they contained miraculous sustenance, Sly leaned back in his chair and focused his misty eyes on the ceiling. "Just when you think things can't get worse, they always do."

Cassie reached for his hand, and he accepted her touch, bringing his eyes back to her face. "Thank you for bringing me with you," she said softly.

"I couldn't go through it alone," he said. "I didn't even think about it. I just knew I needed you with me, and I knew you'd come."

Their eyes locked for a moment, and Sly brought her hand to his face, pressing a kiss on the palm.

The activity and noise in the cafeteria brought their thoughts back to harsh reality. "Let's take some coffee up," he whispered.

Hours passed and night fell, and most of the family went home to rest. Only Sly's parents remained at the hospital with them, taking turns sitting with Sasha. Cassie and Sly dozed on each other's shoulders, half-awake, half-asleep, waiting for any word at all that could tell them if Sasha would survive.

It was close to four in the morning when Cassie woke from her half sleep. Sly was resting on her shoulder, his breathing a restless, dreamy rhythm against her neck. She closed her eyes and prayed that God would not choose today to take Sasha. If He did, neither she nor Sly could ever forgive themselves. And she didn't want Sly to be hurt like that a second time. It wasn't fair.

But nothing had been fair lately, she thought as a wave of anger stirred within her. She remembered her phone call with Amanda, the hostility she had conveyed. But Sly had come to her—not Amanda—when he needed someone. She would not abandon him in his grief this time. He was not married yet. She wondered if it was too late for her.

The fear of pregnancy swelled inside her again. But somehow it wasn't as frightening as saying good-bye to Sly again. If she had to make a choice...

Sly stirred, his rough, stubbled jaw moving against her shoulder. "Hi," he whispered, his eyes narrow half-moons adjusting to the bright hospital lights. "I dreamed I was with you. I'm glad it was real."

She smiled and lifted his hand, pressed it against her face. God, how she loved him. "Your mother's been in there a long time," she said softly to avoid waking Jasper, who slept in a chair beside them. "Let's go relieve her. I want to see Sasha."

Nodding agreement and stretching life back into his limbs, Sly took her hand and led Cassie to Sasha's room, where they found his mother asleep in a chair. Without disturbing her, they went in, separated and stood on either side of the old woman, whose face was lit by a dim light over her head. "Grandma?" Sly whispered, stroking the coarse gray hair pulled back from Sasha's face. "Can you hear me?"

The little woman under the sheets didn't move. Her breathing was shallow and less steady than before. Cassie leaned toward her. "Sasha, it's us. We're worried about you." Tears crept into her eyes and she pressed her fist against her mouth. "Oh, Sasha. Don't let go. We need you."

Sly mumbled an expletive and ruffled the soft waves of his hair. "I'll never forgive myself. I was so mad at you that I risked her life. I let my temper explode and everything came out. I had no right!"

Cassie straightened, her attention now solely on Sly. "Don't do that to yourself, Sly. We both thought she was stronger. She had practically guessed, anyway," she said in a broken voice. "If I hadn't been so selfish, so afraid—we had come so close to getting back together, Sly. If I had just followed my instincts, Sasha wouldn't be lying here."

Their eyes locked, then Cassie's dropped back to Sasha's wrinkled face. "I know Amanda doesn't want you near me," Cassie choked out, unable to find the courage to stop herself. "But I'm not ready to let you go, Sly. I need help. When I called you last week, I was going to tell you..."

"You called me last week?" Sly asked suddenly, but Cassie wasn't surprised that he hadn't been told.

"You were in the shower. Amanda answered."

Sly's lips became narrow lines across his face and he focused his eyes on the ceiling. Muttering something she couldn't hear, he brought his eyes back to hers. "That must have been Saturday night. She was there when I came out of the shower. What did she tell you?"

"That you had decided to marry her. Frank had told me already, so it didn't come as a shock."

"Frank?" His brows knitted, and he frowned at the rail as if sorting out a puzzle. "They're in this together," he said as though it had only now become clear. "Cass, they lied to you. Frank told me that you and he were getting involved. And Amanda knew I still cared for you. She lied to you, Cass."

New hope swelled in her heart and spilled out of her eyes. "Oh, Sly. If only there were another chance for us. I'm so afraid. But being careful means losing you. And I don't think I can stand that again."

Sly caught his breath, a deep frown cleaving his forehead. His eyes were eloquent, but he made no effort to speak. He just stood against the rail of Sasha's bed, gazing at Cassie as if he wasn't sure he had heard what she'd said.

Sasha's trembling hand balled into a fist on her chest, and suddenly she flung it out to the side and hit Sly in the stomach. "Are you just gonna stand there like a fool, or are you going to answer her?" she cried in a hoarse voice.

"Sasha!" Cassie cried, wiping the tears away as Sly stepped back, stunned.

Martha woke up and sprang to her feet. "Sasha! Oh, thank God!"

"Not now, Martha," the old woman said, impatiently waving her daughter-in-law away. She turned back to Sly, pulling herself up to face her grandson. "This girl just told you she loves you and wants to come back to you. Didn't you hear her?"

"Sasha, lie down," Martha begged.

"Hush!" Sasha ordered, still looking at Sly. "Answer me, Sylvester!"

Sly's eyes were on Cassie. "No, I didn't hear her say she loves me."

Sasha muttered something at the ceiling, then turned back to Cassie. "Spell it out, child. He needs to hear it straight out."

Cassie's eyes were smiling, though they were still welled with tears. "You were faking, weren't you, Sasha?"

"Never mind!" Sasha croaked. "Do I look like a dying woman? Tell him, Cassie!"

Sly came around the bed to face her. "What you said a minute ago. Were you saying . . . ?"

"I love you, Sly," Cassie cut in, new tears springing in her green eyes. Sly's arms came around her, clinging so tightly that she thought her bones would crush, but the sacrifice would have been worth it.

"Finally," Sasha exclaimed, knocking at the bedrail to move it. "Now get out of here and talk it out. It's time for this nonsense to be over!"

Martha rushed to her side then, and Sasha pushed her hands away. "Oh, just help me out of this bed so I can get home and rest. All these people poking and blubbering over me . . ."

Cassie turned back to the bed. "Should we tell the doctor that you're all right after all?"

Sasha waved a dismissing hand. "He's so smart, let him figure it out for himself," she said with a half grin. "Let him think he cured me. Now go! And when I see you two again I don't want to hear anymore of this divorce nonsense. I'd hate to have to die to get you two back together!''

Realizing she would do just that if the situation called for it, Cassie and Sly left Martha to handle the old woman who had the wits to outlive them all. Sly took Cassie into the hall, turned her toward himself, and said, "Let's find someplace to be alone. We have a lot to talk about."

And Cassie knew that she had no choice but to tell Sly the truth about her fears.

Chapter Twelve

The sky was the pinkish gray of twilight before dawn as they drove down the gravel driveway to the Farrell home where Sly's three brothers and his sister-in-law were sleeping.

"Give me five minutes," he promised as he got out of the car, "and I'll have the house empty."

Cassie followed him in and laughed aloud when he dashed up the stairs, stopping midway up. "Wake up, everybody," he shouted. "Grandma's all right!"

Doors began to open, and Sammy was the first to come out, eyes red with sleep. "She woke up?"

"Sure did," Sly said. "Wants to see all of you as soon as you can get there." An immediate chatter began as everyone scurried around to get dressed.

"Aren't you going to tell them she was faking?" Cassie whispered.

"And risk having them stay here? No. They're so smart, let them find out for themselves," he said, mocking Sasha's voice, and they laughed against each other.

Within minutes the house was empty except for Cassie and Sly, whose smiles melted as they stared at each other as if the moment of reckoning had come.

"Now," Sly began in a soft, anxious voice, sliding onto the kitchen counter and pulling Cassie between his knees. "About what you said in Grandma's room—if you didn't say it for her benefit, I need to hear it again."

Cassie couldn't hide the warm rush of feeling on her face. Nothing mattered anymore except Sly's smile. "How could you not know that I love you?" she asked, "I've spent the last two weeks crying my heart out for losing you again."

A frown knitted his brows. "You didn't lose me," he said. "You practically sent me on my way."

"I didn't want to," she said. "I wanted to marry you."

Sly's eyes narrowed, and he studied her as if he'd never figure her out. "You had a funny way of showing it. You said I was rushing you. Your job seemed to mean more—"

"It was an excuse."

"You needed an excuse not to marry me?" His eyes reflected fresh pain, and she wanted to set it right.

Cassie sighed and stepped out of his grasp, hoping she could think more clearly if she had some distance. "Sly, have you ever been so afraid of something that even thinking about it tore you inside out?"

Sly watched her for a moment, then dropped his eyes to the counter between his legs. "Yes," he said, finally. "I feel that way every time I think of the possibility that I'll have to go on without you." He brought his eyes back to hers and slid off the counter, taking her by the shoulders. "Look at me, Cass. What are you afraid of? All I want is to make you happy. All I want is a future with you and the children you can give me."

Cassie shook free of his hands and clutched her head. "Don't you understand? *That's* what I'm afraid of! That's exactly what I can't give you! Sly, I'm afraid of having another child. I can't bear the idea of another failed pregnancy!" The words, once out, seemed even more dreadful than she had imagined.

Sly's face changed as a new understanding washed over him, and a jagged sigh tore through his chest. "Cassie, look at me," he said, taking her face in his hands. "That will never happen to us again. The pregnancy was normal. It was just a difficult birth that killed the baby. It was a horrible, miserable thing, but it won't happen again."

"You don't know that," she whispered, wishing with all her heart she could believe him. "I don't think I can do it again. And I can't deprive you of the family you want."

"*Deprive* me?" he repeated. "You already have deprived me. The biggest deprivation of all is life without you, Cass. I don't have to have kids. All I want is you."

Cassie turned away from him. "What about Amanda? *She* could give you children. What happens when we're old and you look back and don't have children or grandchildren, and you realize that you had the chance to have them with someone else?"

"I'll have you," he said.

"You'll *blame* me!" she blurted. "You'll resent me!"

Sly banged a fist against the refrigerator, and the bottles inside clashed against each other. "Then give up, damn it!" he shouted. "Throw it all away because of something that you think might happen! If you can't trust me to love you and be happy with you for the rest of your life, then you deserve to be alone!"

Cassie's throat felt tight and dry, and new tears flooded her eyes. Raking a hand through her hair, she went to the door and started out it.

"Cass, don't go," Sly said in a softer voice. In seconds his arms were around her, and he was turning her to face him. His voice came in a whisper against her forehead. "You make me so angry sometimes. All I want is to love you. I don't care about kids if I can't have you. Amanda and I are finished. That was why I had asked her over that night. I had decided that with or without you I couldn't settle for less. You're the only woman I've ever loved, Cassie. Can't you understand that?"

Cassie looked into his eyes, so intense, so painfully honest, that she wanted to believe him. "I think so," she whispered.

"Then it's settled. After we remarry, am I moving to New York, or are you moving to Chicago?"

"I'll move right away," Cassie said, wiping back her tears. "I hate my apartment, anyway."

"Thank God you didn't say it would take time to arrange." Sly sighed, slinging an arm under her knees and lifting her. "I'm not good at reading between the lines."

"Where are you taking me?" she asked as he pushed the kitchen door open with his back.

"To our room," he whispered, "where I can live out some of these wild dreams that have kept me from getting any rest for the past two weeks."

Cassie nuzzled Sly's neck, and he moaned under his breath as he carried her up the stairs into the room that awaited them. Laying her gently on the bed, he stretched himself above her, memorizing her face as he anchored her. "When I saw you yesterday," he whispered, tracing the outline of her lips with a finger, "it was like the sun came out for the first time since I saw you last."

"I was so glad to see you," she told him. "I wanted to die without you."

"So did I," he said. "I kept thinking how close I had come to bringing you back with me. I went over and over it all in my mind, but it never made sense. If I'd known—"

Cassie was pulling his shirt from his jeans, and she rolled him over on his back and slid it over his head. She licked one brown nipple, painting it with fire, drawing it to a point as he sucked in a breath. Her fingers traced the waistline of his jeans, making his stomach dip as his muscles tightened. Her lips coasted down his stomach, and slowly, she unzipped his pants and brought his body to life.

A feeling of adventure overwhelmed her as she experienced her power over him, moving across his body with the single goal of fulfilling his needs.

As he watched motionless on his back, she sat up and pulled her shirt over her head. She watched the color of his eyes change as she unhooked her bra and let it fall. Her breasts were full and budded, and she took his hand and brought its palm to one creamy mound.

"You're driving me crazy," he whispered, reaching for her with his other hand, but she pulled out of his grasp.

She stood up and pulled her pants down her hips, over her knees, and stepped out of them as he watched with hooded eyes. Standing naked before him, she raised her arms, pulling her hair into a pile on her head, only to let it fall as he raised himself up to look at her, his face eloquent with longing. With a teasing smile in her eyes, a smile she had learned from him, she let him take her by the hips, his mouth alighting on her stomach as she arched against him, arms closing around his head. He lifted her with his arms tightly around her hips, his teeth closing over a nipple, his tongue shooting a shiver throughout her.

When she was under his power again, he loosened his hold of her, letting her slide down his body until he reached her lips, devouring her mouth with passion that could not wait. Her legs went limp, and he lowered her to the bed, his breath ragged against her ear. When he pulled back to remove his clothes, she reached for him, desperate for the union. His black hair tumbled into his eyes which were luminous with desire, creating a fantasy that he swore to fulfill, only to create another as he slid up her thighs, the rough stubble of his jaw brushing her skin where it touched.

He took her with desperate, welcome force, drawing her with him down the rapids of desire, snatching the world from beneath her as they whirled through a trembling, vibrant adventure that would bind them for life or do them in. Gasping for breath, she clung to him for better or for worse, knowing when she released him that he would anchor her for the rest of her life.

They trembled in the aftermath, clinging to each other for fear it had been a dream. And then they slept, their dreams merging, drawing from reality.

It was fully morning when the sound of cars on the gravel drive woke them. By the time they were dressed, the family had come inside and Jasper was raving.

"I'm telling you, Martha, she's senile."

"Oh, hush!" Sasha shouted. "Leave an old woman alone."

"Haven't you ever heard the story of the little boy who cried wolf?" Jasper ranted.

"Never," Sasha declared.

"Well, you should!" he retorted. "You taught it to me!"

Sly and Sasha came down the stairs, biting back their smiles to avoid setting off the wrong person.

"And you two had better be here to tell us about a reconciliation!" Jasper bellowed, pointing at them.

"At least we agree on that," Sasha mumbled.

Sly scrubbed his jaw to hide his grin. "We're getting married as soon as possible," Sly said.

"Good! Now can we please get things back to normal around here? Mama," Jasper said, taking Sasha by the arm, "I want you to lie down."

"Lie down? I've been lying down for two days. You're the one who needs to sleep. Fussing and worrying over me—"

Jasper threw up his hands in exasperation. "Senile," he muttered, bolting up the stairs.

Martha managed a smile. "She had us scared to death," she told Sly and Cassie. "But I suppose she knew what she was doing if it brought you two back together."

"You didn't upset the doctor too much, did you, Grandma?" Sly asked.

Sasha grinned, her gray eyes twinkling. "He's still trying to figure it out," she said, laying a shaking hand on Sly's shoulder. "Now you two will help me when Jasper declares me insane and has me committed, won't you?"

"He wouldn't dare," Sly laughed. "You're the sanest one I've ever known."

"What would you have done if it hadn't worked, Sasha?" Cassie asked.

"I knew it would," Sasha said. "I figured if a lie could almost bring you back together once, then a bigger lie would do it again. Besides, I needed a little vacation," she said, covering her mouth with a gnarled hand and laughing.

Martha shook her head and followed her old mother-in-law into the kitchen where the others waited, leaving Cassie and Sly alone.

"Can we do it without lies from here on out?" he asked, drawing her closer to him.

"I think so," Cassie whispered. "As Sasha once said, sometimes a lie is only the truth in disguise."

"I'll take it any way I can get it," Sly drawled, kissing her again.

Epilogue

April sun bathed the hospital room in golden color, and Cassie smiled at her husband lying asleep on the narrow sofa next to her bed, exhausted from the night's work. She could not sleep, for the wonder and joy of what they had just done together was greater than her fatigue. Sly had helped her through what she had feared more than death.

The door pushed open, and Sly awoke instantly as the nurse came in with a small, moving bundle. "Thought you might want some company," she said in a soft voice.

"I'll take her," Sly said, springing up immediately and cradling his arms for the baby. He held her like a fragile treasure that might break with the raising of his voice, and smiling, the nurse left them alone. "Look at her, Cass. She looks just like you. Red hair, and that cute little nose..."

"Let me see," Cassie said, pulling herself up in bed. Carefully, Sly laid her in Cassie's arms.

"What I've always wanted," he whispered over the baby as he sat on the edge of the bed. "A little duplicate of you. She's perfect."

Cassie held out a finger for the tiny little hand to grab and pull into her mouth. "The next one will look like you," Cassie said with the deepest feeling of serenity she had felt in months.

Sly's eyes left the baby and lingered on his wife's face. "The next one, Cass? You really mean that?"

The baby sneezed, and Cassie laughed and whispered, "Bless you." Then she looked at Sly, who was still studying her eyes. "I mean it, Sly. I'm not afraid anymore."

He shifted on the bed and framed her face with his hands. "I love you, Cass. You don't know how scared I was when you went into labor last night. I knew you'd been scared since the day you found out you were pregnant, and the thought of anything going wrong just—"

"It didn't," Cass told him, eyes welling. "I'm so glad it happened the weekend of the reunion. It took the choice away from me. And you made me feel so much more sure."

He kissed her over the baby, his fingers gently molding her smooth cheekbones, and she wondered if she would ever get over the light, fluttery feeling in her heart whenever Sly touched her.

A commotion in the hall drew them apart, and they both turned toward the door.

"I don't have germs!" a hoarse, raspy voice was saying. "That baby wouldn't be here if it weren't for me! They even named her after me!"

"This is why I wanted to bring you back to Langston to have the baby," Sly told her with a thread of laughter while he pulled himself off the bed. "We couldn't possibly have a baby without Sasha to inspect her."

"She's my great-granddaughter, young lady," Sasha was shouting to the nurse. "And I'm going to see her or die trying!"

"You'd better go tell them to let her in before she fakes a heart attack." Cassie laughed. "It's time for little Sasha to meet this notorious great-grandmother of hers, anyway, don't you think?"

Sly beamed and pressed a kiss on Cassie's lips again, but the baby began to squirm and let out a hungry scream at the top of her lungs. Almost in synchrony, a crash sounded outside the door, and Sly threw back his head and laughed as he rushed for the door. "What am I going to do with my women? I'd better drag Sasha out of the corridor before I have to drag her out of jail." He glanced heavenward, shrugging, the most delightful grin on his face. "I wonder if it's possible to be happier," he said as he opened the door to share with Sasha the most precious gift they had ever exchanged. The gift of life. The gift of love.

Take 4 Silhouette Special Edition novels
FREE

and preview future books in your home for 15 days!

When you take advantage of this offer, you get 4 Silhouette Special Edition® novels FREE and without obligation. Then you'll also have the opportunity to preview 6 brand-new books —delivered right to your door for a FREE 15-day examination period—as soon as they are published.

When you decide to keep them, you pay just $1.95 each ($2.50 each in Canada) *with no shipping, handling, or other charges of any kind!*

Romance *is* alive, well and flourishing in the moving love stories of Silhouette Special Edition novels. They'll awaken your desires, enliven your senses, and leave you tingling all over with excitement...and the first 4 novels are yours to keep. You can cancel at any time.

As an added bonus, you'll also receive a FREE subscription to the Silhouette Books Newsletter as long as you remain a member. Each issue is filled with news on upcoming books, interviews with your favorite authors, even their favorite recipes.

To get your 4 FREE books, fill out and mail the coupon today!

Silhouette Special Edition®

Silhouette Books, 120 Brighton Rd., P.O. Box 5084, Clifton, NJ 07015-5084

Silhouette Special Edition

★ AMERICAN ★ TRIBUTE ★

AMERICAN TRIBUTE

Where a man's dreams count for more than his parentage...

Look for these upcoming titles under the Special Edition American Tribute banner.

LOVE'S HAUNTING REFRAIN
Ada Steward #289–February 1986
For thirty years a deep dark secret kept them apart—King Stockton made his millions while his wife, Amelia, held everything together. Now could they tell their secret, could they admit their love?

THIS LONG WINTER PAST
Jeanne Stephens #295–March 1986
Detective Cody Wakefield checked out Assistant District Attorney Liann McDowell, but only in his leisure time. For it was the danger of Cody's job that caused Liann to shy away.

AM-TRIB-1

Silhouette Special Edition

AMERICAN TRIBUTE

AMERICAN TRIBUTE

RIGHT BEHIND THE RAIN
Elaine Camp #301—April 1986
The difficulty of coping with her brother's
death brought reporter Raleigh Torrence
to the office of Evan Younger, a police
psychologist. He helped her to deal with
her feelings and emotions, including love.

CHEROKEE FIRE
Gena Dalton #307—May 1986
It was Sabrina Dante's silver spoon that
Cherokee cowboy Jarod Redfeather couldn't
trust. The two lovers came from opposite
worlds, but Jarod's Indian heritage taught
them to overcome their differences.

NOBODY'S FOOL
Renee Roszel #313—June 1986
Everyone bet that Martin Dante and Cara
Torrence would get together. But Martin
wasn't putting any money down, and Cara
was out to prove that she was nobody's fool.

MISTY MORNINGS, MAGIC NIGHTS
Ada Steward #319—July 1986
The last thing Carole Stockton wanted was to
fall in love with another politician, especially
Donnelly Wakefield. But under a blanket of
secrecy, far from the campaign spotlights,
their love became a powerful force.

COMING NEXT MONTH

THE PERFECT TOUCH—Rita Rainville
Psychologist Jana Cantrell was hired to help reduce the stress at
Wade Master's company. She soon found that Wade was causing
her own tension level to rise.

A SILENT SONG—Lacey Springer
When Gray Matthews rented the apartment upstairs, Allegra
determined to keep her distance. She couldn't risk getting
involved with a man who might discover her true identity... or
could she?

ONCE UPON A TIME—Lucy Gordon
Bronwen was a young widow struggling to care for her son, until
an Italian prince rode into her life proclaiming her son his heir
and capturing her heart as well.

REASON ENOUGH—Arlene James
Captain Vic Dayton had very specific ideas about decorum. Coral
defied every convention that Vic held dear, yet it was her
charming lack of inhibitions that eventually melted his heart.

CROSSWINDS—Curtiss Ann Matlock
Amanda was lovely, spirited, sensual... but she was a minister!
Cole found himself inexplicably drawn to her, but could a man
like Cole actually fall in love with a preacher lady?

BEWITCHED BY LOVE—Brenda Trent
Sweet, vulnerable Ashlyn Elliott was a witch. Playing the sexy
witch Ravenna on television created a dual life for Ashlyn, and
Davis Chamberlain found himself falling in love with both of her.

AVAILABLE THIS MONTH:

SOUNDS OF SUMMER
Annette Broadrick

SWEET SEA SPIRIT
Emilie Richards

BEFORE THE LOVING
Beverly Terry

SHADOW CHASING
Debbie Macomber

LOVERS' REUNION
Terri Herrington

THE COURTSHIP OF DANI
Ginna Gray